## OTHER WORKS BY JUANA CULHANE

*Bird on the Wing:*
*Travels of the Self*
(NY, Spuyten Duyvil, 2011)

*The Celestial Monster:*
*Two Collections of Stories*
(NY, Spuyten Duyvil, 2008)

*The Revelations of Dr. Purcell:*
*Stories from the Life of a Psychotherapist*
(West Virginia, University Editions, 1992)

"The Shadow of the Cat Goddess"
In *The Theory and Practice of Self-Psychology*
(NY, Brunner Mazel, 1986)

"The Headless Toy Soldiers:
The Terrorization of a Patient by Unsoothing Introjects"
In *Psychotherapy and the Terrorized Patient*
(NY, Haworth Press, 1985)

# The Tattered Lion

*Stories of a Man through
the Eyes of a Woman*

## Juana Culhane

Spuyten Duyvil

*New York City*

"Twig Under the Door," "Stone Rubbings," "A Trip To Die For," "Zotz, The Bat God" (was "Stranger in the Bat Cave"), and "Embrace in Stone" (was "Scream of the Peacock"), *The Celestial Monster: Two Collections of Stories*, New York, Spuyten Duyvil, ©2008. Reprinted by permission.   "Family Fairy-Tale," "The Revelations of Dr. Purcell," and "Stories from the Life of a Psychotherapist," West Virginia, University Editions, ©1992. Reprinted by permission.   "Unforgivable Woman, the Perfume" (was "The Braid"), and "Apparitions" (was "Tricksters"), *Bird on the Wing, Travels of the Self*, New York, Spuyten Duyvil, ©2011. Reprinted by permission.

Cover art by Panama Campbell

ISBN 978-1-933132-97-6

Library of Congress Cataloging-in-Publication Data

Culhane, Juana.
The tattered lion : stories of a man through the eyes of a woman / Juana Culhane.
p. cm.
ISBN 978-1-933132-97-6
I. Title.
PS3603.U56T38 2012
813'.6--dc23

2011048311

The Tattered Lion

## TABLE OF CONTENTS

## AUTHOR'S NOTE

For a long time, my stepsons, Brian and Kevin, whom I love and admire, have wanted me to write a memoir of my long marriage to their father, Shamus, James.

I cannot fully comply. Instead, in this volume, I have compiled stories previously written as fiction—all influenced or haunted by my late husband.

Some have been published in other collections, some are different versions of published stories, even under a different title.

Directly or indirectly, literally or figuratively, they paint a portrait of a man and of part of our life together.

It is written
upon my beloved's grave
        "No Stone Unturned"

Let him now
        lift himself up

And standing by my side
        smile

Unperturbed at last

*Author's Note to Cave of the Patriarchs*

This story is inspired by William Blake's prints of Babylon's exiled King. It is also inspired by Blake's following poem:

### The Sick Rose

O Rose, thou art sick.
The invisible worm,
That flies in the night
In the howling storm:

Has found out thy bed
Of crimson joy:
And his dark secret love
Does thy life destroy.

# CAVE OF THE PATRIARCHS

The three patriarchs huddled together in front of their cave, wondering why fate had treated them so badly. They were old, sick, in rags, their nails like talons, their deaths already in the past. Looking around, their eyes full of horror, all they could see was tall grass, jagged rock. Nearby was a wild rosebush with many thorns and one red rose—its petals were slowly withering.

All three had known a girl called Rosa. All three had desired to possess her. Keith, Rosa's father, needed a superior extension of himself to conquer hearts; Earl, her father-in-law, needed to be her lover; James, her second husband, needed proof of her loving *only* him.

"It's not our fault," Earl began, "She was ripe for the plucking."

"What a dirty old man you are," Keith intervened. "You just wanted to show me up because, I, the bald little man, ended up with a beautiful wife and three gorgeous daughters. I, the uneducated misfit, ended up with a life of adventure in Latin America."

Earl rebuked him, "It was you who were jealous of me. I had the looks, style, brains, knowledge—everyone gravitated to me, from our days as hoboes, to my winning a rabbi's virgin daughter, to my siring a genius boy."

James screamed at the two of them, "It was men like you who ruined my wife Rosa so that I could never trust her."

"Oh, shut up. What nonsense," Earl snarled, "What a coward you are. Even now you can't enjoy that you had Rosa for almost forty years, and towards the end you were still whining she never proved her absolute love for you."

Though he'd been listening carefully, Keith said nothing. He couldn't help thinking that James had little to complain about except for a seductive mother who French-kissed him at three and dumped him at five. Of course, it was sad that his beloved father was always away at sea, but though James would deny it, he was probably greatly responsible for three failed marriages before meeting Rosa. Earl, on the other hand, had lost his hearing, his teeth, to a brutal father when he was a youngster. And he? It was a long story.

Keith was born in New York to an unmarried, live-in housekeeper and a chauffeur from a different household. Unable to care for her baby, the mother took him to

England to be brought up by her sister and brother-in-law. Five years later, after she and the chauffeur married, she rushed to England to claim her son, to bring him back to New York. On the ship, on the way back, all of Keith's hair fell out; he was in terror; he thought he was being kidnapped by a witch, stolen away from those he thought were his parents. His mother was mortified, at first hurt, guilty, then angry. Matters worsened when, even after consulting physicians, his hair never grew back, except in unsightly wisps. In addition, Keith became surly, introverted, not even trying to ingratiate himself. His mother became angrier and angrier, punishing him at every turn. His father was indifferent, doting on subsequent children, babies he could hold and win over from the very beginning.

When Keith was twelve, he was yanked out of school and forced to work full-time as an errand boy in local businesses. At fourteen he became a choirboy in the Catholic Church. For the first time since England, he felt appreciated; the priests thought he looked like a beautiful cherub, bald, short, fine-boned, delicate in his behavior. His deep timidity they interpreted as modesty, humility, and adoration of them.

One day he came home late from choir practice. His mother confronted him.

"So, what have you been up to? Hanging out smoking

on street corners?" Her sharp features were even more outlined upon her chalk-white skin, her voice strident, as she wiped her hands on her apron, emerging from the kitchen.

Tears rolled down Keith's cheeks. He was stooped, holding his body tightly together, "Mama, I'm hurt."

"What! What have you been doing?"

Like a small child, he pulled down his trousers, by now wailing loudly, "I'm bleeding, look at what he did!"

For a moment, her face softened, "Oh my God, you're injured, what happened?" She ran up to him and held him, helping him to step out of his pants, "Tell me, what on earth happened?"

"Father Paddy did it!" Keith clung to her.

She backed away, horrified, slapping him to the floor as blood continued to run down his bare legs, the backs of his legs, "How dare you lie about our saintly Father! What have you really been doing?"

Keith stopped crying. Picking himself up he ran into the bathroom, locking himself in, eventually falling asleep curled up on the floor. At dawn, he washed himself, crept into his room, dressed, put his last pay in his pockets, and he left home forever. He slept on park benches, eventually joining up with other homeless young boys. Some called themselves anarchists, others nihilists, all angry, split off from family, from society. Finally he hooked up with young men who took to the rails, calling themselves hoboes. They rode all over the USA, hopping on and off trains at will. Sometimes, in friendly towns, they performed odd jobs in exchange for food, a bed, a shower. Most often, they stayed together near railroad stations, cooking hustled or stolen food over open fires, reading out loud from books they'd found in the garbage. One member recited poetry from memory or from poems he'd composed himself. His name was Earl. Keith was in awe. He's never felt more stimulated to learn, to read, more and more, quickly digesting books of all sorts, from *Popular Mechanics,* geography, travel, to world literature.

Several years passed, until one day, full of disparate pieces of knowledge, Keith decided to get out of the USA, to seek his destiny elsewhere. With the help of books, he taught himself how to handle a radio; he applied as a radioman to Pan American Airways and asked to be sent to Latin America. Of course, he had to lie about his education, and he passed their examinations with flying colors. Ending up on top of a mountain, north of Mexico City, he guided air traffic and dispensed warnings about the weather. Later he worked on the island of Cozumel, able to go by launch to the mainland from time to time for recreation. He fell in love, married, and sired three daughters, while continuing to travel throughout Central America. Rosa, the oldest, became his protégé when she was still a child. Being bright, malleable, she was perfect for carrying out his fantasies of becoming omnipotent, of rising above being a baldy, a little runt, a nobody.

More years passed. Restless, idealistic, he wanted to do his bit against fascism. He moved the family to the U.S. He once again performed well on exams, entered the Air Force as a captain, and was sent to France to help rebuild airports as they were bombed out. He came home in 1945 as a colonel. After traveling all over the U.S., the family finally settled in New York in 1948. In time, Keith looked up an old friend from his hobo days. Earl had one child, a son three years older than Rosa, a genius and a scholar. The boy was as symbiotic with his father as Rosa was with hers. They were easily maneuvered into a marriage, both fathers relishing the idea of the coupling of the brain and beauty. But Keith's wife had not been heeded. In fact, her protestations were ignored. She feared for her daughter's welfare, not trusting what she sensed about Earl. This marriage between the twenty-year-old boy and the seventeen-year-old girl, broke Keith's family apart. It was never the same again.

• • •

Back in front of the cave, James was still furious at Earl, calling him a coward, but he was too debilitated to confront him physically—all he could do was screech in a reedy voice, "At least I had emotions, feelings. You, on the other hand, were just a decadent left-winger, a radical, believing in free love, which just meant a free-for-all sex fest, even with your wife's friends. And look how stupid you were, idealizing Stalin up to the moment he was unmasked and even promoting that debauched writer Maxwell Bodenheim, who was eventually murdered."

"God, you're such a prude!" Earl yelled, "Look at yourself, running after Rosa when she was still married—as a matter of fact, you were married too—panting after a girl half your age, you, all of forty-eight, middle-aged, already getting paunchy."

"We loved each other. We had passionate sex like we'd never had. *I* was the one who believed in her higher self. *I* encouraged her studies. *I* gave her stability."

"Yeah, yeah, all the while brow-beating her with your jealousy, your possessiveness. At least if I had been her lover, her partner, she could have been herself, experimenting, growing and maturing naturally, when she was ready."

"Christ almighty how can you talk so lightly about a woman's body, her  honor? How could you even imagine yourself her lover, your son's wife?"

"Grow up! Rosa was your fourth wife—you just legalized your desires, your fickleness, and what about the fact that each wife was younger than the last, ending with Rosa, twenty-four years younger than you." Earl continued with venom, "You were old enough to be her father while you made use of the best years of her life. Did you ever think about the hell you put her through in the end, taking care of you at home the last five years? Don't you remember all your collapses from congestive heart failure, your diabetes? Don't tell me you forget ending up incontinent, bedridden, and having refused to go to a nursing home." Stopping to take a deep breath, Earl then asked, "Did you ever thank her, tell her she was a great woman, that you believed in her *whole* self, had faith in her?"

James answered, almost in a whisper, "She did it out of love for me, you moron, and I deserved it."

"Ha, ha," Earl mocked, "We don't deserve anything; we're not owed anything—after all, there needn't have been any life at all, just boulders, rocks. We're here on earth; we fill ourselves with what we can of knowledge, beauty and love; and then we die. If we're lucky, we leave behind some delicacies of our own making for others to enjoy."

"It's much more complicated than that," James retorted, "We must help others, save them from themselves sometimes, nurture and mend them, heavy-duty repairing sometimes. Rosa had the misfortune of being precocious growing up and backwards once she was grownup. She was like a colorful piece of clay that needed shaping, formation, structure."

Earl pulled some tufts of matted hair out of his long, white beard. "What shit! Who do you think you are, Pygmalion, God?"

"You think you haven't done the same?" James began indignantly, "Using your John Barrymore looks, your charismatic articulateness, to weave webs around your admirers, your followers—all those youths you induced into joining your little army of anarchists. And look at what you did with that son of yours, never seen with a toy, only with you, never seen with other children, except in school, always only with you." Seeing Earl's face sag downward, James became energized, "And when he won a scholarship to M.I.T., he ends up hiding under his bed, unable to function without you—he was your creation, your puppet."

Earl became quiet. He was remembering many things. He prided himself on being a superb teacher, mentor. In his son's case, maybe he had overdone it, not realizing until too late that the boy had gotten totally attached to him. Of course, it was part of his reason for pushing the marriage of the youngsters—it would give his son companionship, a sexual partner, a semblance of normalcy. And as far as Rosa was concerned, she's the one who worshipped him, her father-in-law, seeking him out for help with her schoolwork, her papers. She's the one who flaunted her beauty, trying to entice him, needing to conquer his affections. He couldn't help but fall for her. After all, they spent much time together, roaming the city together, walking through all its parks, rummaging around in secondhand bookstores, talking endlessly in quaint bars. He had no idea that she was so innocent, not, as yet, having consummated her marriage, not knowing her own body. As James said, she went from precocity to backwardness.

"Isn't this what we've been waiting for, wanting, for so long? Earl murmured to Rosa as he held her tightly. In a fit of passion, he'd swung her onto his lap as he sat on the edge of her bed.

She didn't know what to say or do, but she knew she wanted to be as far away from there as possible. She was frightened, almost disgusted, by his gaunt nakedness. As she returned from her last day of high school, he had awaited her wearing only his robe, which he soon unsashed as he followed her to her room. She felt like an ineffectual child, guilty about getting into a mess, fearing consequences, deeply embarrassed, wanting it all to go away, perhaps wishing she could be saved by a higher power.

"It doesn't feel right," she whispered lamely, weakly making a move to get off his lap. He was shocked; where was the young woman of the world who looked up to him so adoringly. He was red in the face, his breath hot, sweet from passion, his hands frantic as he tried once again to kiss her. But with all her squirming, he ended up kissing only her nose, her chin. Finally, she stood, awkwardly by his side, not knowing what to do. He looked at her in the face, frowning. Then nodding, as if realizing something, he stood up, and with his head lowered, he left the room, quietly closing the door behind him.

After this incident, he kept his hearing aid turned off most of the time, pretending to be totally absorbed in his work as a poet, translator, proofreader. Many years later, he died excruciatingly of emphysema, with his ever-loving wife by his side.

James was reminded of the day and night he was in his death throes. Rosa lay by his side as they listened to Vivaldi's Double Concerto. She burnt candles as, one by one, his organs gave out, thrusting his body into heaving convulsions. But though unable to speak, he felt he was only in a half-sleep, not a coma. Before he lost his speech, had he told her he loved her, trusted her? He couldn't remember.

Keith had been sensing everything quietly, listening

with this third ear, seeing with his third eye. He himself had died suddenly at sixty-two of coronary thrombosis, unfulfilled, his dreams of conquest through his progeny destroyed. But now he wondered if perhaps his greatest creation, greatest accomplishment, *was* the life he'd led, with all the hurdles he'd overcome. Maybe he *was* a kind of a hero. He hadn't had to take his daughter's life to form it into what he wanted. It's strange, he thought, if Earl hadn't been so bitterly disillusioned with the world, he might have appreciated the poetry that he wrote, the poetry he could have written, and might have put the energy of his lust into it. And James, if he could have overcome his fears of abandonment, he might have seen that he had what most men don't, the undying love of his chosen woman.

As the three men crouched on all fours, they looked at each other and wept. There was nothing else to think, nothing else to be said or to do. They turned their faces toward the rosebush, with its solitary rose. If they could have they would have stood upright and applauded. They would have, cheered at what they saw. The rose petals were withered no more; they were velvety, vivid. All was well.

# TWIG UNDER THE DOOR

He hadn't shown up.

How cold it was. How silent. No one was around. She snorted, lowering her head further into her coat collar. She half sensed where her feet were going. She didn't care. They could go wherever they pleased. She wasn't even looking. Before long she did look, and there in front of her was *his* apartment, all lit up. Why not? He was loved, wanted, while she stood in the black night, in the even blacker shadow of a tree. As she began to turn away, something writhed, crunched under her feet. Stooping, she picked it up, caressing the crooked twig. It was then that she became aware of a shrunken, huddled man standing not too far away. He was watching her. It seemed to her that his arms and legs trembled to her touch, shuddered at the movement of her hands upon the cold scarred wood.

Crossing the street, she disappeared into the apartment building. Up the stairs, avoiding the elevator. Quietly, quickly—his floor, his hallway, his door. An ear to the door. Merry voices, melodious and high-pitched yelps of glee. A family, a young family. Abruptly, she jammed the twig under the door, ran down the stairs and out of the building, continuing to run till she reached the corner. As she caught her breath, she sensed more than actually saw the raggedy man nearby.

All afternoon, she'd waited. All evening, too. Waited by the window, by the rustling silk drapes. Waited on the couch, staring at his giant golden flowers in his Jensen's crystal vase, listening to Schubert's Unfinished Symphony, sinking into its ominous forlornness. Why hadn't he come? He had called the day before saying he'd be able to get away, to sneak away for a few hours. Had she sounded too light, too busy, though she'd said it would be great to see him? But then, he sounded casual, too, as if any day would do in which to see her. She couldn't have said that, not only was she willing to give him all her time, but also all of herself; suppose he didn't want her that much? She'd be totally exposed, out on a bare limb.

Before leaving her apartment, she had ripped apart one of his flowers, stuffing the dying leaves and petals into one of her coat pockets. As she walked slowly toward the Hudson River, she touched them once again. They were still warm, soft.

At last she reached Riverside Drive. The wind blew upon the trees. They bowed a little. She felt as if this desolate place awaited her—the whirling wind, the rippling river, the emptiness. She stopped for a moment. She was not alone. She heard a delayed echo of her own footsteps. Not daring to look back, she walked on, her face hot. Was it fear? No. She was waiting for something to happen. She walked on for a few more blocks.

The river flowed, reflected lights bounced upon it, the wind blew hard, and still, nothing happened. She should be relieved, but no, something *must* happen. Her hands formed fists deep in her pockets as she muttered, "Come on, do what you must!" The footsteps behind her quickened, grew louder, as if she'd been heard. "Come on, be brave!" she laughed to herself, beginning to walk faster, digging her heels into the sidewalk, straightening her shoulders, listening. The footsteps following her became louder and louder. "It won't be long now," she muttered. Loud, firm, faster and faster—footsteps, her heartbeat, all resounding together. "Come on, garnish this dreadful day!" She almost laughed out loud at her own pompous words.

At last the footsteps were upon her. A presence was close by. She half closed her eyes looking down. What a squat shadow—his was large, looming ever larger and larger. "Do it, do what you will!" she felt like screaming, but only a whisper came out. "For God's sake, don't be timid!"

Suddenly a touch on her body, the merest, most tentative touch on one of her buttocks, barely felt through her coat. She flung around, eyes bulging, neck muscles bursting. Seeing the same man she'd seen on Central Park West, she snarled, "Get away from me! How dare you!" The man recoiled with astonishment and just stood there in front of her, his thin baggy trousers and rumpled cloth jacket flapping in the cold wind. She turned, continuing to walk, her whole body burning; unable to resist looking back, she saw the man walking slowly away in the opposite direction, a hunched shadow in the night. Beginning to shiver violently, her shoulders slumped downward, her hands unfolded in her pockets—the petals and leaves had withered, becoming slimy and cold. She threw them into the wind, watching as they swished away, falling apart, disintegrating, merging with the rest of the debris on the street.

# Underpinnings

As Joanna's taxi approached her apartment building on Riverside Drive, she saw James's imperious, tall figure on the sidewalk—long black coat, black fedora, big-chested, pacing back and forth, hands in his pockets. Much earlier, she'd waited and waited. He hadn't shown up. She'd assumed he couldn't get away from his wife and little sons, so she'd accepted an invitation for drinks at the Pierre Hotel with an old friend, Marvin. They had never been lovers, they never would be, but they could do or say anything to each other that came to mind. But how stupid of her to have drunk too many Bacardi cocktails; why hadn't she had faith that James would show up eventually! But how could she have—he'd stood her up so many times. She'd thought she would be able to endure the plight of being "the other woman," with no rights. She loved James so much, almost swooning at his first touch every time they met—passionate, assured, yet so terribly needy, almost dangerously so. "Don't tease me! Please, don't tease me!"

he'd almost cried the first time he'd kissed her. Sometimes she wasn't certain whether she'd had her own orgasm or whether she'd been absorbed, enwrapped in his. It didn't matter—her whole being was inflamed, satisfied.

Once inside her apartment, without removing his coat and hat, he pushed her up against the wall, shouting, "You're drunk! You told me you loved me. Why are you doing this?" Before she could answer, he slapped her. "Why didn't you tell me you wanted to play around! I've turned my life upside down for you!" His face was flushed, his beautiful delicate lips twisted.

Joanna lunged forward a little, one side of her face burning. "You're married. You're still sleeping with your wife, enjoying a family life. I left Nat, my friends, stopped taking a lot of modeling jobs, because you disapproved!"

"Some work, those half-naked jobs of yours!"

"I have to make a living. After all, you employ nude models—that's how you met me, remember?"

Giving her another push, snorting, he slammed out of her apartment, never discovering that she had no underpants. She had forgotten that she couldn't find them in Marvin's suite when they'd played a game of Dare. James, of course, would never understand, would never condone the playfulness of acting like children in a sandbox or a mud pile.

# STONE RUBBINGS

The comforting crow of the rooster had ceased long ago. Dawn had come and gone, and now the hot sun engulfed everything in sight. Nothing and no one moved quickly in the archaeological site of Chichén Itzá, as if all were content and never eager for escape. Even the dust, lifted slightly in a random breeze, quickly settled. Joanna's arms, neck, and legs ached as she stood holding the large, white umbrella over the tall figure of her husband. His black crayon stroked the moistened rice paper on the stone faces and bodies of ancient Maya warriors. (In the early days of the opening of the site, it was possible to obtain permission to do stone rubbings.) As he worked, she was as mesmerized by his face as she had been the first time he'd drawn her. Only now, a few years later, the soul-melting tenderness was gone. There was a narrowing of the violet eyes, as if they were reluctant to reveal the flashing flecks within, the effort twisting one corner of his mouth downwards. She shivered. Then she asked, "How do you know where to rub so as to get the original design and not just cracks and bumps?"

Not looking at her, he answered in a rich, soft voice, "I know what I'm looking for. I know the Maya."

She persisted, "If you didn't know, you wouldn't be able to do a rubbing?"

"It'd be harder."

Joanna looked around at the vast, open plaza, not one person in sight, only the carcasses of temples belonging to a lost world, a world that had belonged to her mother's ancestors, a world she knew very little about, having long ago become a total New Yorker. Timidly, she asked, "Will you be all day today, too? My neck and everything are getting really tired!"

He laughed, still not looking at her, "Take a rest anytime you want. I'll just get a redder face! After all, it was all *your* idea, the umbrella thing to protect me."

"I know," she murmured, becoming determined to keep her arms up a bit longer. She'd been diagnosed with a joint disorder not long before. "Stress is a contributing factor," her doctor had said. "Stress over whether to run away or stay and fight," he'd added cryptically. At the time she could only laugh.

After a long silence, still keeping his eyes fixed on his work, he murmured, almost purring like a big cat, the way she loved, "You know, last night your whole body, even every strand of your hair, from its roots all the way to its ends, smelled of the mangoes you'd eaten all day."

She giggled. The night before had been one of many perfect nights in their large hotel room with its rustic wooden furniture, the whirling fan far overhead on the beamed ceiling—naked, perspiring, lingering, everlasting caresses, kisses. Nothing rushed, nothing abrupt, that is, until he had spoken, "I'll bet there isn't one person who hasn't loved doing this to you." No anger, no accusations, only a sadness, like the sadness within his plea the first time they'd kissed, "Don't tease me. Please, don't tease me."

She hadn't responded then, just as she hadn't the night before as they'd lain under the circling blades of the fan. His behavior was strange, considering the circumstances. But then, so was hers. They were both acting as if they'd never received that dreadful news only two days before. "There's an urgent telegram for you, senora, from England!" the hotel clerk had whispered to her. It was from her sisters. "Father died. Funeral five days. Please come." She had rushed to their room, wanting to be held by James, to hear that everything would be okay, that the world was still there.

As soon as he read the telegram, he had shocked her by beginning to cry inconsolably. He'd only met her father twice, though he'd heard stories about his adventures in

Latin America from her.

"Why did he leave me?" James lamented. "He was always going off to sea, always gone!"

Slowly, she'd realized he was talking about his own father, who had returned home only to die of tuberculosis of the spine.

"*She* chased him away, that fucking excuse for a mother!" James exclaimed.

Joanna had wanted to shake him, beat on him. She had wanted to shout, "Hey, it's *my* tragedy now, my loss!" but she didn't. She couldn't. She could only cry with him as he clung to her.

"I'm sorry! I'm so sorry to go on like this; I just can't help it!" he moaned.

She'd thought that at least he'd agree that they must leave immediately for the funeral, but he'd insisted that he had to finish his rubbings. Totally dismayed, she'd thrown up all over him. He'd shouted, "What's the matter with you? You're acting as if you've lost the one and only love of your life!"

He was immediately remorseful. Embraces, kisses, hours of making it up to her, making love desperately, as if to penetrate every one of her pores, to suck out, to lap up all of her essence. She had later sent a telegram to England, saying they'd be there as soon as possible but would miss the funeral.

Now as she once again surveyed the dusty plain of Chichén Itzá, she wondered what it was about the Maya that captivated James. "You're part Maya, aren't you?" he had asked in the elevator the first time they ever set eyes on each other, not knowing that she was on the way to his studio to be his model for the day.

"Yes, on my mother's side."

"I knew it! I could tell because of the square corners of your forehead, your temples."

Putting down the umbrella, Joanna asked, "May I see what you're doing?"

"Of course, but it's only another one in the series you're familiar with!" he exclaimed, reaching for her, drawing her to his side so they could gaze at his rubbing as if with the same eyes. Profile of a warrior, mouth open, fierce eye, plumed headdress.

"You see how grand he looks—searching for his place in the universe, ready to fight to assure himself he exists and that the gods *want* him to exist, *need* for him to exist!"

Joanna was reminded that none of the drawings he'd ever done of her looked in the least like her; they had all depicted heroic-looking women, almost masculine, with eyes that looked far off, toward the heavens.

"Have you ever done a rubbing of a live person— is it possible to do?" Joanna asked, in a low voice that trembled a little.

Turning to look at her, his eyes gleaming with mischief, he purred in his big-cat voice, "What a great idea! Whatever made you think of that?"

# THE DEFROCKING

Joanna awakened lying down on a strange couch. She sat up, startled, not remembering how she got there. Dr. Hart sat nearby, "Shhh, don't panic. You fainted in my classroom; I carried you in here. Are you feeling yourself again?"

"I guess so." Joanna was uncertain. All she could remember was sitting with others at a conference table listening to one of Dr. Hart's patients. His name was Michael and he looked like a young Peter O'Toole. He was explaining what had led to his being defrocked.

"Are you on any medications that could have led to your fainting?" Dr. Hart lit his pipe. He was calm, almost aloof.

"Only my usual anti-inflammatories, for my rheumatoid arthritis, but I'm used to them; I've been taking them for about ten years."

"I see. I never would have guessed you had any illness," he added gently.

"It's only a slow-moving type," she said, feeling more

assured that she didn't look like a total fool, "I've had it since my twenties." Joanna began to get up.

"No, sit, sit, don't you want to explore what happened to you?" She frowned. "Don't worry," he explained, "I have time, an hour or more."

Joanna felt compelled to stay. She should get to the bottom of things. After all, she was in training as a psychotherapist. But it was difficult to shake her sense of embarrassment, even though she knew that she wasn't required to be without flaws, without vulnerabilities. But she was required to *know* her defects, to understand them.

Dr. Hart looked at her expectantly.

Joanna began, "I was not aware of feeling anything special as I listened to Michael. I was just mystified as to why he wanted to be a priest in the first place, and I wondered why he seemed to display no shame."

"You were shocked by his open admission of debauchery?" Dr. Hart's thick eyebrows rose high on his forehead.

"Not really. I was puzzled."

"You expected him to be perfect, to not falter?" he asked.

"No, of course not!" she insisted.

"In any case, Michael is leading a different life now," Dr. Hart beamed, "He's completed five years of treatment, he's married, expecting a baby, and above all, he was able to withstand the scrutiny of all of you!"

"I know, I know, but it's not the morality issue," Joanna argued, "It's something else!"

"Do you faint often?" he asked softly.

"No ..." but she was hesitant.

"Tell me about another time you fainted." He put down his pipe and sat back in his ample chair.

"It wasn't much, a non sequitur that doesn't fit anywhere," she answered.

"Tell me about it." His voice was firm.

"Well, my physician and I had a great medical relationship for many years; he saw me through many a crisis, health-wise and marital."

"Yes?"

"One time, when he stepped out from behind his desk, extending his hand to bid me goodbye, he ended up embracing me. When I froze in place, one of his hands guided one of mine towards his groin. That was the last I remember. The next thing I knew, I was looking at his rumpled hair, his face full of mascara, his expression of total dismay. I was in a fury; I actually felt violently angry. I rushed out of his office. Soon after, by letter, he referred me to another doctor, a specialist, a rheumatologist. I never saw him again."

With eagerness, Dr. Hart asked, "What connection

do you see between then and now?"

"I'm still certain it's *not* my judging some immoral act. It's something else." Joanna was still adamant.

"You see your doctor as behaving immorally?"

"Well, wasn't he?"

"You tell me; you're the one who may not allow for lapses."

"No, it's not that, I told you!" Joanna was irritated.

"Okay, okay—" Dr. Hart leaned forward, his elbows coming to rest on his knees, his body looking short, squashed, his balding head overlarge. "Let's backtrack. I'm sorry if I rushed you. Perhaps I was thinking in simplistic terms. So, the fainting was *not* caused by medications, nor by issues of morality. Are there any big stresses going on in your life at the moment?"

Joanna took a deep breath, her soft features relaxing into her usual expression of serenity, "Well, something good has happened. You could call it a *good* stress. My husband James and I are together again after a trial separation."

"May I ask why you separated in the first place?"

"I needed time alone. James had become so possessive—imagine, he was even jealous of my father, who had just died!"

"Oh?" Dr. Hart's forehead wrinkled up as he slowly sat further back in his chair again, subtly stretching his body upward.

"Yes, James felt betrayed by my mourning Papa; he thought it was too long."

"Was it really?"

"Yes, probably. I had a breakdown of sorts," she giggled a little. "It was funny in a way! Once, I hid out in a closet all day! Apparently, poor James looked for me all over the apartment and the neighborhood, too. He was so upset!"

"Did you consider *that* being too possessive?" Dr. Hart asked, laughing a little.

"Oh, no, of course not! I just suddenly remembered that incident. No, what I considered too possessive was his jealousy, his thinking I was loving someone else more than I loved him."

"Did you love your father more than James?"

"Not really! I was just as surprised as James that I reacted the way I did to Papa's death—I was *so* overwhelmed by anguish, by anger, both clashing together!"

"Anger?"

"Yes, he died so unexpectedly! He wasn't sick. He wasn't old! He never said goodbye! Also, he died not long after James and I finally got married."

"Did you feel responsible for his death?"

"I think I did! I did love James more than I loved

him," Joanna said, as tears screened her eyes.

Dr. Hart said nothing as he picked up his pipe and relit it, puffing loudly. Then he spoke, "Now back to the anger. You do know, don't you, that you were angry not just because he died, but because he died before something could be expressed, no?" Then he added, "This is not uncommon!"

Joanna nodded but was quiet. Dr. Hart continued, "Perhaps you had a resentment you hadn't voiced." He took a deep puff on his pipe. "Is it possible this resentment could be along the lines of—well, let's say, similar to your reaction to Michael's betrayal of his followers, who worshipped him, or similar to the rage you felt when your doctor took advantage of your vulnerability?"

"No, no, nothing like that, nothing so crude!" Joanna was horrified. "Papa and I had a special love, totally unique! We weren't just father and daughter. We were better than friends or companions. We were more like a mirror image of each other ... in a mirror of gold!"

"Sounds almost too ideal!" Dr. Hart began laughing and ended up coughing as his face turned red. Finally, in a choked voice, he continued, "So ideal, so safe, and yet so dangerous—oh, what disappointments, what disillusionments can result!"

A stillness descended upon the room as both Dr. Hart and Joanna gazed out the window at the cooing pigeons as they fluttered their wings at each other. Finally, Joanna sighed audibly, looking around the room for her things. She just wanted to go home to James. She felt a great urge to make it up to him, not only for having asked for a separation, but for having gone through with it. She wanted to go home to his embrace, to his calling her "my pussycat," to a long kiss that would slowly envelop her, encompassing all of her, beginning with her entire face.

# A FAMILY FAIRY TALE

I had been working with a family for a few months and was beginning to worry about being able to be of any help. The family consisted of a father, his wife, and his two sons. The wife was the sons' stepmother. Although the sons' mother was not actually present, she was very much there, with all of them. The father was a vital, successful man in his fifties. He had known power and admiration. The sons, aged twenty-two and twenty-five, were floundering, trying to find themselves. The stepmother was about forty, and she was a medical research nurse. The mother had not remarried though she had been divorced for about ten years—she was alone and she demanded attention from her sons. She came from a famous family of circus performers specializing in high-wire feats, but she herself had not followed in their footsteps. She also was in her fifties, like her ex-husband.

It was difficult to pinpoint the problem. Each member

of the family just seemed to yearn for appreciation from the other members. However, the father and his wife wanted to move on with their lives, while the sons seemed to be waiting for something that was not, as yet, forthcoming. They had all come into treatment at the request of the father, who wanted to "clear the decks" before proceeding with his life.

One session, there had been such a violent fight between the father and his sons that I had felt like leaving the office. Of course, I didn't; I was determined to understand and to try to help. The previous night, I had had a dream, a strange dream set in another time, in another place. I couldn't remember it clearly, but when I awoke, I had had glimmerings of a fairy tale that involved an omnipotent king, an old, banished queen, a wicked stepmother, and sons on a quest. The dream images excited me. I decided to let my imagination go and to actually create a fairy tale. I would let my feelings, about each character and what each conveyed to me, guide me in my search for the basic truth of this family. And so, I sat down and wrote my fairy tale, knowing in the back of my mind that I had personal reasons for wanting to help. The family was very much like my own in that I'd become a stepmother to two young boys when James and I married so many years ago.

Once upon a time, there lived a king in a far-off kingdom. It was a small kingdom, but it spread itself out across the whole top of a fertile mountain. There were trees and flowers everywhere, and, where there were dry patches of earth, beautiful rocks had been placed in decorative patterns. The king loved his trees and his flowers, but his collection of rocks were the most precious to him. "What joy to make the earth bloom with inorganic, everlasting life," he would cry out as he gazed lovingly at his rock garden.

I wondered why I thought of using the symbol of a rock garden. I remembered an article about the culture of Japan and how, during World War II, refugees, being moved out of Tokyo, were forbidden by the authorities to bring their beloved rocks with them on the trains. The authorities insisted that the rocks took up too much space and that the space should be for people. But, to many of the Japanese, the rocks were a presence in themselves and deserved their own space. Even now, in modern Japan, some rocks sell for thousands of dollars. I also remembered an obscure philosopher-biologist, Hans Jonas, who, writing in the 1960s said, "If permanence were the point, life should not have started out in the first place, for in no possible form can it match the durability of inorganic bodies."

After remembering these small details, I continued

writing my tale.

The king lived in one wing of a big, stone castle, with his new queen, who did not have any children, and with some of her family. In another wing lived his old queen, and in yet another wing lived their two sons.

The old queen was a little mad; she wandered around in her chambers repeating, "I'm the queen, I'll always be the queen!" She had always been a little mad. She used to move the king's rocks around when he wasn't looking, and once had even tried to break some of them with a small hammer. Other times, she had played hide-and-seek with some of the rocks, all over the castle. She had enjoyed watching the king's rage as he frantically ran everywhere to retrieve parts of his collection. She would laugh and say, "You see? Does everyone see? It is not me who is mad—it is him! Do you not see how his veins are bursting out of his forehead?"

When the king had obtained a new queen, the old queen was furious. She ranted endlessly to her sons about the unfairness of the fates. She screamed that she should be more respected, that in her family of yore there had been five famous knights.

The sons loved their mother. They felt her frustration and wanting to soothe her, they asked, "How can we become knights, too, so that we can vindicate you and carry you up high over everyone' s heads?" The old queen would always answer, "Demand your knighthood from your father, the king!"

The king's name was Leopold, and his new queen was called Leona. The two sons did not yet have a firm name. They would get it when they achieved knighthood. In the meantime they were called Uno and Dos. The sons found the king very baffling. He wouldn't tell them how or when they could become knights. In time, though, Uno and Dos came to believe that they should be knights just because they were the king's sons. They didn't think they should have to wait or to do anything special. After all, they were past eighteen years of age. Whenever possible, Uno or Dos, or both of them, would press their demands upon their father, but they did so timidly, for they did not want to anger him.

There were some times when the sons forgot all about what they deserved as their birthright, and they merely enjoyed being with Leopold and Leona. Together, they would go for long walks all around the mountain, looking for rocks for the king's garden. The sons liked watching their father make marvelous forms and structures upon the barren patches of earth. They had sometimes even thought of finding a very special rock for their father, to please him, but they were so afraid that it would not be perfect enough that they never even started to hunt for the special rock by themselves. Not being able to do what they secretly wanted to do, they became more strident in their demands. "Make us knights, and we will honor you so much that you will love us!"

The king heard them, but he was not impressed. He did not believe that he was empowered to make them knights. He believed that his job was done. He had led them to their manhood, and now they had to learn how and where to find their knighthood. He had not had his kingdom given to him. He had fought many battles, been terribly wounded, and had finally won his mountaintop. Now and then, he would look at his ravaged body in a looking glass, ponder over the long scar that seemed to sever him in half, and say to himself, "Was it worth it?" But then he would remember his rock garden, and he was certain that it had been worth it. The rock garden was not only a symbol of his innermost pleasure in himself, it was a gift to God, *his* father, who would gaze down upon it and beam gloriously.

During his long reign, the king proved himself to be quite generous. He bequeathed all of his valuables, including the rock garden, not only to his sons but also to the young offspring in his queen's family. Leopold proudly told Uno and Dos what he had done and was surprised when they became angry and shouted. "How could you give away to others what belongs only to your blood relations! When are you going to accept us as your only true sons?" The king did not understand. Then he thought that they were only being greedy or that the old queen had been urging them on more than usual. He did not yet see that they hungered to be knights so that they could feel strong and loving instead of being racked by envy.

Now and then, the king would give his sons parts of his rock garden to reassemble in the patio of their wing of the castle. He wanted them to appreciate and love him. He couldn't show his love more earnestly than by giving away what was the most precious to him. Uno and Dos seemed pleased by this; they smiled and hugged their father, but the stricken look still remained in their eyes. It was this look that particularly disturbed Leona. It was the sad appeal of a helpless infant, and it touched her deeply, especially since she still mourned being childless.

Uno and Dos did not often invite Leopold and Leona to their wing. They didn't avoid doing it. They just thought that Leopold and Leona wouldn't be interested, and anyway, Uno and Dos felt they had little to give, especially since they kept being denied their knighthood. However, Leopold and Leona were always gratified when they received an invitation from Uno and Dos, and they would eat and drink with great relish, in unison with them, as if they were all of the same generation.

Most of the time, if Leopold and Leona wanted to see Uno and Dos, they invited them to their own wing. Uno and Dos often complained that they were invited as guests, just like anyone else, and not as Leopold's sons. "Why can't we get the golden keys to your rooms and come and go as we wish? Aren't we deserving enough?"

One day, a messenger arrived with a letter from Uno asking what time he was to arrive for dinner at Leopold's. Leopold and Leona were undressed and resting in bed. Leona sent the messenger with a note naming the time that had been prearranged by Uno and herself many days before and returned to bed.

Suddenly, the bells at their gate rang out loudly. Leopold and Leona flung on their robes as their servant announced at their bedroom door that Uno had arrived. Leona was furious. With her huge robes flapping around her, she ran to confront Uno. "Why do you not respect our time arrangements?" she yelled. "You're not due for another two hours!"

Uno was pale, but he stood very straight, very still, and he retorted with a quiet hatred in his voice, "It's about time that you and our father accept us into the fold!" And stiffly turning on his heels, he left.

Leona was so incensed at how she had been provoked for no good reason, that she burst out at Leopold, "Why don't you give your sons what they want so that they will leave us in peace!"

"I cannot give them what is not mine to give. I cannot give them joy in themselves. They are not ready to be knights. When they are ready, they will become knights," he answered with finality.

"But if you make them knights, they *will* have joy in themselves."

"No, that is not how joy in oneself is born." And that was that.

Many days went past, and soon, Uno and Dos seemed friendly again. One day Leopold and Leona were invited to visit Uno and Dos. The king's birthday was to be celebrated, and the sons had invited many of their friends from other mountains. Spirits were high and all seemed well. Leona thought that perhaps Uno and Dos were no longer obsessed with being made knights by their father and that they were working on their own projects so as to become worthy in their own right. She went out into the patio to once again look at the beautiful rocks that Leopold had given them over the years. She immediately saw many gaps in the original designs; some of the rocks were missing. She could not believe her eyes.

She found Uno and Dos and asked, as calmly as she could, hoping that it was all a mistake, "Where are the rest of your father's rocks? Have you placed them elsewhere?"

Uno felt like a scolded child. He looked around at all of his friends, and a great embarrassment flooded over him, followed very quickly by rage. He answered,

"What does it have to do with you? The rocks were given to me and to Dos, and we can do anything we like with them!"

"No, you cannot. They are part of me!" bellowed Leopold upon hearing Uno's words. "By sunup I expect all of the rocks I have given you back in my rock garden. You do not deserve them!" And Leopold grabbed Leona's arm and left.

Uno and Dos were mortified to be so criticized. They had expected their father to defend them against their stepmother. They had had no idea that the missing rocks were *that* important. After all, they were not destroyed. They were just misplaced somewhere. But Uno and Dos weren't sure what had happened to them. Vaguely, they remembered that they had lent them to someone. In any case, they had to comply with their father's order: find all the rocks and return them. Many days passed again, but the king could not forget how insignificant his rocks appeared in his son's eyes. They seemed not to understand how important they were to him. They were himself, they were his life, they were his gift to God.

"Don't you see?" urged Leona, "They want you to place them above all else in life, above me, of course, but above yourself, and above God. They are truly tormented souls in need of everything, in order to feel that they have a little something!"

"What have I done to them? How have I failed, that I should have such sons?" And the king and the queen wept together. They wept for Uno and Dos and their destiny, for themselves, and for all imperfections.

One day, a festival was planned by many distant kings. They were to honor Leopold for his courageous deeds and for his beautiful, fertile mountaintop, but above all, they were to celebrate his rock garden.

Uno and Dos were happy for their father. They wanted to be part of the festivities. After all, they were his only true sons, of his very own blood. They asked if they could be made knights at the same time that he, the king, their father, was being honored. Leopold thought for a moment, frowning deeply, and then said, very quietly, "No, this is my day, my time. You will have your own day, in time. But it is my dearest wish that you come and celebrate with me." Uno and Dos could not believe that they could be treated so; they felt ostracized and unloved.

The day of the festival came, and there was much rejoicing. Leopold was happy. Leona was happy for their life together, but she couldn't help but wish that she had been able to give him a child. As the day passed, Leopold became worried. His sons had not yet appeared. He called for a messenger to go and fetch them from their quarters. The messenger returned, saying that they were gone, and so were all of their possessions. Leopold and Leona rushed to the castle to see for themselves. It was true. They were gone. All that they had left were two rocks of their father's, which they had not returned to him when they had been ordered to do so.

Leopold and Leona climbed up into the tower. They almost ran up the steep steps. They looked at all the roads leading away from the castle. Suddenly, they spotted Uno and Dos, far away, almost out of sight. "We must go after them!" gasped the queen, starting down the stairs. "They are your only children!" The king stopped her, hugged her violently to his chest, his whole body trembling.

"No, we must let them go! They must seek their knighthood elsewhere!"

"But can you live with the thought of never seeing them again?" cried Leona with anguish.

"One day, when they create their own garden, perhaps not of rocks, perhaps of other essences, and offer them to God, wherever I may be, I will be reunited with them."

I put down my pen. There was a tightness in my throat, tears in my eyes. What steps should I take now? Should I interpret the fairy tale to the family? But what good would that do? They might understand themselves, and each other better, but it wouldn't bring any of them what they wanted. Certainly not now. Perhaps that was the point, each had to keep on living his or her life, struggling in his own way, searching for what each one needed, whenever and whereever.

All they could expect from each other was a modicum of empathy for what they were experiencing. Suddenly, I exclaimed within my head, "but why *all*?" Empathy *is* everything, to feel what's in other people's heads and to care in a sympathetic way is the uniting force in all people. It certainly isn't blood, having the same genes. As I felt a union with the family I knew it was time to look upon my own house with different eyes.

My heart beat rapidly, my cheeks felt flushed. I felt intensely happy. I felt as if I had received a valuable gift, as if I had been embraced. I knew I was ready for the next session with the family. I didn't know exactly what I would say or do, and it didn't matter at all.

# THROUGH THE DOOR
## NEVER OPENED

As soon as dinner was over, the struggle would begin again. While eating and drinking, making love with their eyes, their words, Joanna and James could pretend they were young, healthy, untroubled. The restaurant was like a small palace, full of paintings, plants, velvet drapes, and candles. The gracious service added to their sense of being special. In their silken clothes, who could guess that he was in his eighties, dying of a congestive heart, and that she was in her sixties, frightened to her very core? Who could guess that in the forty years they'd been together, each had almost died many times from loving too much—or perhaps it was from loving too little. To give your all is to drown the other.

James reached for her hand on the tablecloth, his heavy, Greek coin ring pressing against her swollen knuckles. "After we separated, have you ever regretted getting back together again almost thirty years ago?

Imagine it's been *thirty* years!"

"Funny," she chuckled, her face golden in the candlelight, "I was just thinking about that time!"

"Oh, what specifically?"

Joanna laughed. She knew he couldn't help challenging her, testing her. "I called you, told you I missed you, that I wanted to see you." After looking at him mischievously, her dimples emerging from her plump cheeks, she added, "You came running within the hour, remember?"

"Of course. You were my wife, no matter what. I told you I never wanted to know what you'd been doing and with whom, but of course I've wondered about it. In all this time, did any of your old boyfriends ever cross our path, unbeknownst to me?"

"No," she answered simply.

He squeezed her hand a little before continuing. "I've been meaning to ask you, but I didn't have the nerve, "In all your years of therapy, did you ever get your father out of your system?"

"I think so. I'm not sure," she said softly.

He squeezed her hand, hard. She winced a little, and he immediately loosened his grip. For a moment, she felt that old fright, that old guilt, as if she had done something wrong, as if she were hiding something. This feeling had never gone away, but knowing that it was irrational, she'd always been able to push it aside.

"Don't worry," he murmured, caressing her hand. "I've learned to act *as if* I'm not an insanely jealous man! By the way, do you remember the book you gave me that evening, when I 'came running' as you put it, T.S. Elliot's *Four Quartets*? Do you remember your inscription?"

"No, what did I say?" she asked enthusiastically.

"You wrote:

> Enjoy the beauty within, especially the end where he begins, 'We shall not cease from exploration ...'"

Joanna sighed. "Well, we've certainly done that, our joint therapy, the fun and fights with the boys, all our trips, the struggles with our illnesses, our surgeries."

"And don't forget our talks, your reading out loud to me, our lovemaking, sharing our work problems, cooking together for as many as twenty people!" James exclaimed, releasing her hand to brush his long white hair away from his rosy cheeks, away from his moist forehead. "Tell me, you must know, what comes *after* those lines about exploration?"

With ease, she recited,

> "'And the end of all our exploring
> Will be to arrive where we started
> and know the place for the first time.'"

James asked, "Do you think that's true?"

Quietly, as they sipped their wine, they remembered how they met, how they began to know each other. The elevator of his apartment building, when he began staring at her. It made her uneasy, though she was used to it. After all, she was twenty-four, sprightly, and looked as if she came from a far-off exotic land. Finally, he spoke to her, "Are you by any chance part Mayan?"

Surprised, she turned to look at him—floppy beret slanted over high round cheekbones and playful light eyes. But it was his small mouth, his sensuous lips that attracted her. She liked his tentative smile, so unlike the sureness of his mustard-colored tweed jacket. "Yes, on my mother's side," she answered. "What made you ask?"

His smile remained tentative. "Your facial bones, your square temples."

And that was that, except that they got off on the same floor, not knowing that he was the artist for whom she was to pose that day. Later, as he drew her entire figure, barely looking at her, he concentrated on the image he was creating on paper. She liked this shyness. She felt her presence affirmed, while at the same time feeling untouched, not intruded upon.

Much later, when they kissed for the first time, he'd pushed her away a little, saying in a tormented voice,

"Don't tease me. Please don't tease me!" His vulnerability suggested suspiciousness, a warning; this frightened her, but only for a moment. Most of the time, he was merely charming, gallant, offering her turtle soup and champagne before they made love for the first time, much, much later. He continued, passionate but without displaying desperation, remaining hungry but never greedy.

Perhaps she should have told James that their separation hadn't led only to dating. She'd also struggled and suffered. Joanna remembered trying to explain their love affair while in group therapy in a weekend retreat in Vermont. She had just finished describing how she and James, in love long before they met, when a scruffy man called out, "Give me a break!" Then, when she tearfully proclaimed how she had failed James by not being good enough, the same scruffy man hit her on the forehead with a crumbled cigarette pack wrapper, exclaiming, "I've never heard so much shit in my whole life!" Joanna had stiffened up, walked out of the room, out of the house, and into the snowy terrain, tormented by fear, doubt, a terrible aloneness, feeling ostracized for being a romantic.

But perhaps she hadn't told James about this incident because at the end of that long day, after a search party led by the scruffy man found her, they had had sex on the floor in a sleeping bag in front of a roaring fire.

Now, sitting in the shadowy restaurant, they looked at each other carefully. He was a little hunched, his lion's chest now concave. She seemed bloated, her skin and muscle separating from the bone. However, the center of her face retained some tautness, elasticity. It was as if some of her beauty had escaped to a tiny island as the rest of her became hopelessly submerged.

Finally, it was time to go home. Cane in hand, James staggered a little as he stood up. Yet he loudly insisted on forgetting the idea of taking a taxi home. He wanted to walk; it was only a few blocks. Never mind that one of these blocks was uphill. Was it possible? Would they ever be able to walk together again as they had so many times long ago, traversing Central Park, Riverside Park, and much of Manhattan?

They began the climb up their tree-lined street towards the Hudson River. James leaned hard on his cane and on Joanna's bent arm. She noticed he'd put on his beret in a lopsided way. Little by little, as they moved upwards, his mouth opened wide, his cheeks drooped and quivered. They stopped for a moment, glancing at each other. "Is this too much for you?" he queried. He knew that though he had lost a great deal of weight in recent months, his leaning on her so forcefully was hard on her sore, weak joints. He hadn't been aware of how much he needed to bear down on her.

"No, not at all! Don't worry! It's so good to walk together." She knew it was strange, but it was only after she had said this that she realized that part of her wanted to run off in the opposite direction, leaving him alone on the hill. It was as if a double-faced being were after her, chasing her, taunting, menacing—a being she'd known all her life, one face was her beloved, the other was a demon. Taking a deep breath through her mouth, her eyes filling with tears, she moved closer to James, squashing herself against his side. She knew she and James had arrived where they had started, knowing the place well, but not for the first time.

# ACCEPTANCE

The hospital nurse informed Joanna that, on New Year's Eve, her husband freed himself from his bed-restraints and naked, ran down the hall yelling, "Let me out of here." Much later, back in his bed, he explained that his four wives had flown in through the window, intent on killing and devouring him. Joanna was both distressed and amused. She was used to James's temporary episodes of diabetic dementia; she pictured him loping down the hall with his long white hair, broad chest, lean loins, and strong calf muscles. He must have looked like what she affectionately called him, "a tattered lion." She wondered what he would have said about his genitals if he had remembered the event, perhaps something like, "The family jewels went a-swinging." But she was deeply perturbed, not only by the progression of his disease, but by the nature of his vision, the paranoia, he displayed. She was the fourth of the succession of wives, the longest lasting one. He could be so righteous, so judgmental when it came to women; he still spoke with such disdain about her early years as a model. She was reminded of a character in a Greek drama, Pentheus, who wanted to stamp out the Bacchae and their ecstatic ceremonies. Perhaps James's hallucination was based on this ancient tragedy; after all he was a self-taught Greek scholar. Hadn't Pentheus ended up hunted down like a wild animal, torn to bits by the passionate forces he feared and denounced?

Approximately two years later, James succumbed to a series of small strokes, which threw him into a coma, but in which he could breathe on his own. Despite her terror of what the future held for both of them, she was enthralled by the expression on his face—beatific, a heavenly beatitude. She wondered what thoughts, what dreams, roamed within his mind. When he awakened, with no apparent damage, he could speak only about the remarkable dreams he'd had. However, he wished to savor them alone before sharing them with her.

One evening, he took her hand as she sat reading in her study and led her into the living room. "I want to tell you about my experiences while I was in the coma." He gently sat her down close to him on the black leather couch. "I actually went elsewhere, body and spirit. Isn't it something—for the first time in my life I had a religious experience. Imagine: me, the iconoclast!" They embraced before beginning to drink the champagne he'd placed on the cocktail table. As Joanna nuzzled against his aromatic, warm neck, she was once again drawn into one of their favorite paintings hanging in front of her—surreal, exotic, a frightened, large bird surrounded by masked priests with half-animal bodies.

Sipping on the champagne, he began, "In the first experience, I'm one of many celebrants in Eleusis, in ancient Greece. It's autumn, the sun is setting, we are all gracefully wrapped in hospital sheets held together by giant safety pins. We stand around an altar where two deities are dancing, she with a necklace of grain, and he with a garland of fruit. They are priests representing Demeter and Pluto. Her necklace winds around her naked body, while his garland cascades down from his head, like a beaded curtain over his nakedness. But I knew something no one else knew—Pluto was being represented, not by a priest, but by the young general, Alcibiades. I'm on a special mission to ascertain if Athens's beloved warrior should be tried for blasphemy."

Joanna chuckled, thinking that if James hadn't been an artist, he would have been a policeman.

"Despite Alcibiades's mockery of all conventional establishments, everyone adored and admired him, even going so far as imitating his lisp, his swaggering walk."

"Were you planning to turn him in?" Joanna smiled.

"No. All I know is that I hoped he would reveal the

mysteries of Eleusis to me, secrets from the beyond."

"Why was this so important to you?" Joanna asked, trying not to guess out loud, not to anticipate answers, the way she was prone to do. Perhaps she did this because she was a psychotherapist, but most likely, she'd always been like this.

"I think I wanted to know the secret of living and dying well. I wanted to know how to love, how not to be afraid. I wanted to know these things from a God, from the Goddess Demeter, who was many things, virgin, mother, crone. She was the creator, the preserver and the destroyer."

"She sounds a little scary to me!" Joanna exclaimed.

"Yes, but she was a God. I could trust her." James's voice choked up, his eyes and nostrils narrowing as he looked at her intently. Was he angry at her? Joanna wondered. He seemed critical of her. Didn't he react this way every time the issue of "trust" came up? She took a long sip of her champagne, "Please go on," she said. She hadn't noticed before that he had brought out the goblets with his family's Irish name and crest engraved on them—bountiful plumes emerging from a knight's helmet and falling to the side of a shield decorated with a trinity of star-shaped flowers.

"After the sinewy dance on the altar," James proceeded, "After Demeter blessed the initiates in a shadowy corner, all the celebrants, except for myself, chanted, danced, embraced, kissed, drinking red wine from enormous cups as they tossed off their hospital sheets. Demeter grabbed Alcibiades' hand and led him to a flower garden surrounded by tall trees standing on guard. I followed. I watched, listened, and waited for Alcibiades. In time, when he was alone, I asked him what he had learned of the sacred secrets. He whispered in my ear, his breath sweet, musty from all his exertions, 'I will tell you because I know you won't turn me in. As of this moment you are *my* initiate. I bless you with the following truths. You never have to fear lying in darkness, in filth, all alone, not even at the end. You will never live the life of a beast. You can hope for an infinitely higher state of being.'"

James turned to Joanna with such an intensity in his eyes, she was both frightened and excited. "Then he added (as he bit into my ear and I smelled blood):

'The secret revelations can only be discovered through things heard, tasted, seen. You must hear *no* evil, speak *no* evil, see *no* evil, ever again. Never."

After a few moments of silence in which they barely breathed, Joanna asked cautiously, "What do you make of it all?"

"Let's wait till I tell you my second experience. Sometimes I think I understand what everything means, and then I know nothing. I think it's all about you, you and me, and our life together. It's all about what I need to know before I die."

Joanna wanted to kiss him long and hard on the lips, biting into them a little but she didn't wish to interrupt. She had never loved him more than she did at that moment. Looking back she realized she had felt the same when she'd fallen in love with him, when, after their first kiss, he'd said, "Please, don't tease me. Never tease me." She loved his innocence, his vulnerability. Little did she know, then, in her middle twenties, how imperious fragility can be.

"In my second dream-adventure I'm in Persia. I am Xenophon, the Greek warrior. I am angry because of the way I've been treated in Athens, with no respect, no appreciation. Gathering up an army of loyal followers I joined up with a Persian general who had also been betrayed, in his case, betrayed by his own family. I was to help him regain his power, his properties. Unfortunately, he was assassinated, his generals arrested. Though I escaped, there I was, one thousand miles away from home, in charge of an army but surrounded by enemies. I was determined to lead my men to safety, to the Black Sea."

Joanna asked, "Did you question leaving home in the first place?"

"Yes, I had allowed my pride, my bitterness to guide me, but let me continue. This is what I said to my captains: 'The Gods are on our side. We came on this mission in good faith to help a friend in need, a man betrayed. We kept our word. We are good. We will succeed in reaching our mother, the sea. My senior captain, now a general, will be in charge of the front line, and I will be in charge of the rear.'

The trek was arduous, crossing deep rivers, climbing up and down snowy mountains, with the Persian cavalry and hostile tribes chasing us. Sacrifices to our Gods didn't help; they didn't melt the snow or stop the north winds from blowing. There was hunger, freezing, snow blindness, even though my men held something black over their eyes and took off their shoes at night to prevent the straps and soles from sinking into their flesh. We didn't kill *all* our sheep for food so that their warm bodies could provide some solace during the long dark nights. We learned how to tie small bags around the feet of our horses when traveling through snow so they wouldn't sink up to their bellies."

James stopped talking, "Am I boring you? You're so still, not even drinking."

"No, I'm totally engrossed, just wondering if this

incredible trek is a metaphor for your life—it's so adventurous, courageous, but so lonely, always searching, never finding."

"Wait, wait, it isn't over." After taking a long breath and more champagne, James continued, "Finally after months and months I heard a giant roar coming in waves from the front line. At first I thought the enemy was attacking from the front. I rode forward as fast as possible to join the struggle. The roar slowly became words, at first distorted. Then I distinctly heard, "Thalassa, Thalassa, the Sea, the Sea!" We were victorious after all. We were back to the sea, from where all life springs. We were back to be soothed, healed, renewed."

James wept and smiled at the same time, not covering his face or turning away. Joanna's eyes glistened as she restrained herself from sobbing also. After all, this was *his* moment. Touching his face, she murmured, "I'm so happy you're alive and well, my dearest tattered lion." She waited till James was ready to speak again.

"As I talk to you, everything slowly begins to make more and more sense." He paused, turning away as if embarrassed. Then he grabbed her hands, holding them tightly, his head bowed. "All that bellyaching for almost forty years about your damaged soul or what I saw as your star-crossed life."

"But I *was* damaged!" Joanna interposed.

"No. Yes, but no—you see how you yourself make yourself out to be bad?" Joanna was puzzled, feeling troubled, but not knowing why. "I've been wrong, so wrong. It's hard to express, as if something new and unknowable is pressing in on me. When we fell in love, you presented yourself to me in all your nakedness, from the very beginning, without guile, young, waiting for life to guide you, and what do I do, the old ogre—I brand you as wicked—what's worse I brand you with a harshness no one deserves."

"Oh my darling, but I've always felt loved by you, cherished, nurtured, no matter what!" Joanna began to sob, to tremble with a violence that surprised her. She pulled at her short, graying hair, forming a spiky frame around her soft features, her facial muscles collapsing downward.

Holding her tightly, he whispered hoarsely into her ear, "I know, I know, that's because you are my Demeter in all her diverse glory. You have been the Virgin, the Mother, the Crone. You have been my true love, and I didn't know it, until now, now that I am an old man, a man near death."

Joanna couldn't move; she couldn't think; all she could do was continue to weep. In all her life she'd never felt like this before.

# ZOTZ, THE BAT GOD

One early morning, James lay on his back, as he usually did, on his side of the king-size bed, in the yellow-bedroom. But this morning was different from any other morning that had been or would ever be. James, clad only in his diapers, looked like a martyred prophet, or like one of his gallant literary Greek heroes, Alcibiades or Xenophon, at the end of his life. His long hair and his moustache and goatee were white and silken. His cheeks were sunken, his mouth slightly open, expectant looking. His large but emaciated ribcage was rising and falling slowly, arduously, bloating up greedily and shrinking downward reluctantly.

"James, dearest James, can you hear me?" his wife Joanna asked, lying by his side totally naked, her voice trembling. There was no response, not even a change in his breathing. Perhaps he couldn't hear her anymore. Perhaps he was in the coma his doctor had predicted. James's eyes had been closed since the night before when a high fever and violent tremors had begun to destroy a life already enfeebled by congestive heart and kidney failure, diverse infections, from the sinuses to the bladder, and wild swings of his blood sugar.

Looking at his long legs, Joanna once again marveled at their beautiful shape, the stretched out, strong muscles of an athlete. In his youth, before he had become an artist, an animator, he had been a runner. Even though she was so much younger, no part of her body looked as good, her joints and her muscles inflamed or atrophied by her chronic rheumatoid arthritis.

Joanna had removed her pajamas the night before and had lain with him all night, her head slightly above his so that her face rested on his hot forehead. She had pressed herself as close as possible to his body without impeding his breathing. They had listened to Vivaldi's Double Concerto all night long, while a single extra-tall candle had flickered on the table, the flame leaping about in a glass lantern casting circular reflections on the ceiling. These mirages had looked like large golden eyes blinking restlessly. By morning the candle had burned out.

Ordinarily, Joanna would have called 911 long ago, the night before, when the high fever had set in. James would have been stabilized or revived at the hospital as he had been so many times in the last five years. They had said goodbye already, many times, always hoping that the end would come at home, in their apartment. But this time, as the fevers had begun, James had asked her not to call for help, that he was tired, that the time had come.

That momentous, unique morning, moving very carefully, Joanna eased her stiff, cold body off the bed, dressing herself in slacks and a shirt, totally forgetting about underwear. She sat down on a chair by the bed, mesmerized by the rhythmic rise and fall of James' chest, by the otherwise utter stillness of his elegant form, even of his patriarchal head. "Are you there, my dearest tattered lion?" she asked almost inaudibly, her voice weak, forlorn, somehow knowing that there would not be, could not be, any response, ever again. It was strange that only a few weeks before, on her birthday, when she had bemoaned her aloneness out loud as she had lain by his side, he had reached out, clutched her hand tremulously, and had said, "Happy Birthday, dear Pussycat!" But now, despite the fact that he could no longer respond, she felt she could sit by his side forever, merely watching his breathing. She could now see why some people didn't want to remove life support machines from comatose loved ones, because, since they were alive, that's all that mattered. Suddenly she sat upright. There was a change in his breathing pattern. James had taken in, swallowed, a long gulp of air and then had held on to it, had not released it, had held it prisoner within his large ribcage. His chest did not fall again. It didn't move at all. James had died. He was eighty-seven. She was sixty-three.

Then, right there, at that very moment, in the yellow bedroom, in Manhattan, New York City, death had grabbed Joanna by the throat, had shaken her whole brittle body, had assaulted her brain, her very mind, and had left her a message, created in the beyond where death usually roamed, forever gathering wisdom from his multitudinous flock. Death had whispered loudly to her that the time had come for her to spread her life out before her and to look at it. He had whispered that her life was made up of six and one-half wispy diaphanous wings, each full wing representing a decade, that the wings were growing out of her chimeric self—a hybrid, hyphenated, many-genomed self, originating with the merger of her English-Irish father and her Mexican, Maya Indian mother, a self born in Guatemala and thereafter traveling far and wide.

Death had then released his hold on Joanna so that she could go about the business of a funeral and a burial. But he never entirely left her alone, ever again. He loomed in front of her, compelling her to know him, so that she could never mistake him for another, so that she would know with all certitude that she would one day be all his, for keeps. Joanna laughed at herself and her thinking. Of course, it was just like her to think in terms of disloyalty, possessiveness, and exclusivity. From way back, she had felt as if she were betraying someone, something, everything.

One night, after the funeral, in a half-sleep, Joanna fantasized she was a young Maya maiden in ancient Chitchén Itzá in Yucatan, Mexico, a site not far from her mother's hometown, in Quintana Roo, Mexico.

She was about to be sacrificed to Zotz, the bat God. First, she was given savory delicacies, a hallucinogenic tea, painted blue all over, and dressed in an embroidered white gown. Then, after she had been laden down with a myriad of heavy jade necklaces, she was half carried from the nunnery to the edge of the cenote, a deep, wide well. Priests in feather headdresses recited incantations to Zotz, hoping he would be pleased with the gift he was to receive, hoping he would let up on the drought. Then, the priests lifted Joanna up, up high just as her father had done when she was little. But, unlike her father, they then threw her into the murky waters below. Joanna enjoyed feeling herself falling endlessly but never reaching the bottom. It was just as pleasurable as rising upward because she had absolutely no control and therefore no concern, about whether she was doing right or not.

Then her daydream took on a life of its own. An emaciated little bat flew right out of the center of the cenote and began to fly north; she knew it was coming to look for her. Upon awakening, Joanna quickly decided to go to visit her sister Dolores in Santa Fe, New Mexico. Dolores had often talked of Bandolier Park and the caves of the brown bats. Joanna just knew the vampire bat was planning to meet her there.

Dolores met her at the Albuquerque airport, and they drove for an hour and a half to her home, not too far from the central plaza of the town of Santa Fe. Joanna marveled anew at Dolores's beauty, who, though only five years younger than she, seemed ten or fifteen years younger, being healthy and having been a dancer in her earlier years. Dolores had the perfect features of a classical Spanish woman. No one would have thought she was part Maya, unlike Joanna, who James had guessed was part Maya the very first time they had met, because of her square temples. He had often told her, over the years, in an affectionate way, that she had such irregular features that she could look beautiful sometimes and simian, monkey-like, other times. She had then understood why she'd always felt so inferior to Anglo-Saxon women. During the long drive, Dolores' black eyes kept glancing sidelong at her sister with apprehension, never being sure of her unpredictable temperament. As the youngest of the three sisters, she had learned to balance caution with a fiery readiness for battle if necessary. Finally, she spoke: "I'm glad we all had that great Christmas together in New York City six weeks before he died. You remember how much he enjoyed the fresh snow in Riverside Drive Park, even in his wheelchair?"

"Yes, and we drank champagne and he had a snowball fight with your husband!" Joanna answered, though she didn't feel like talking. "By the way, how is your Nick doing? Last I saw, you were doing fine together?" All three sisters had been married more than once. Nick was Dolores' third husband. James had been Joanna's second.

"Yeah, it's still good. Very comfortable. Nothing like what you had with James, so glamorous, exciting! You traveled the world. We hiked the mountains and camped out!"

Finally arriving at Dolores's and Nick's townhouse, Dolores ran around quickly to lend an arm to Joanna, who didn't absolutely need the help, though it eased her stiffness and lifted her spirit. Later, at the dinner table, Dolores said, still in a benevolent mood, "We know you really want to be alone, so its just as well we both have to go to work! But promise me you'll be careful no matter what you do. I don't like what you told me about hearing a voice telling you, "Join me, if you dare!" And look, don't get mad at me, but you seem vague, remote—are you still taking Xanax?"

"Only once in awhile now. Don't worry," Joanna answered calmly, though she suspected she should stop taking the anti-anxiety pills altogether.

In bed the next day, when she was alone in the house, Joanna began to envisage the cenote into which she had been thrown in her daydream. Though she had never reached the bottom, she had seen the maze-like paths, the underground lakes, the brackish water, the dead gardens. No wonder the vampire bat had flown away. She loved savoring the idea she had concocted, that he was coming to meet her. She vaguely wondered why she had invented a vampire bat instead of a gorgeous bird or just a spirit of some kind. She knew it had something to do with a very primitive, very deadly, perhaps murderous need deep within her, with which she was not in touch, as of yet. But perhaps she had invented a vampire because of her Maya heritage, because she was so intrigued by their ancient custom of offering their own blood, and that of especial others, in order to be able to have the privilege of communing with the Gods. Upon getting up at noontime, Joanna put on white, flowing, cotton pajamas and a few strands of turquoise beads borrowed from Dolores's jewelry box, feeling a surge of mischievous power as she did so. Dolores wouldn't like it, but she would accept it. Then, after she patted a deep blue eye-shadow on her eyelids, and after leaving a note that she'd be back late, after dinner, and to not wait for her, she went out, rented a car and drove to Bandolier State Park.

Soon, she was walking on a winding path to the ancient dwellings of the Anasazi, knowing that the bat caves were on the other side, at the far end of the park. Stopping to rest on a bench facing the cliffs, she listened to the distant echoes of visitors' voices, hearing their footsteps as they climbed the cliffs, and went in and out of cave-like rooms. She felt their enthusiasm as they communed with the ancient people, the Anasazi. She wondered if these Indians could be related to her ancestors, the Maya, way, way back. Suddenly, the cliff walls began to lean down towards her, her eyelids becoming dead weights, her brain feeling drugged. She lay down on the bench she'd been sitting on. Soon she could feel the prickliness of the ants underneath her back, her buttocks, her legs. Deep below the bench, she felt the ancient tensions within the earth, the fissures, the cracks, the eruptions of ash, gases, dust, cinders and hot lava. Joanna remembered the night before James died. She'd been awakened by a violent shaking of the bed. James had been having convulsions. His whole body it seemed, was being torn asunder by an invisible force, perhaps by the full extent of his turbulent, tormented life, his passionate longings which had become fixated on Joanna, his fourth wife of almost forty years. Perhaps, though, some of the underground rumblings even came from her own fixations.

Joanna must have fallen asleep on the bench, in the park, because when she awakened, it was almost dark. The moon was very low in the horizon; all the visitors had disappeared. She walked up the main path towards the long house and she climbed up the many steps to the bat cave. She wondered why it was that she was so spry and limber, having no hint of impairment. It was as if it was another time, when youthfulness was taken for granted, when getting old was unthinkable. Though her disease had taken many years to cause any disability, she'd been diagnosed with rheumatoid arthritis a year after she and James had met, when she was twenty-four and he was forty-eight. Her disease was an auto immune disorder in which her own body's defense system mistakenly attacked itself, causing chronic inflammation. Joanna chuckled, thinking of that saying about being one's own worst enemy.

Joanna crept in, toward the restless flappings of the bats in their cave, and stood quietly in a corner, able to see black on black. She could smell a heaviness, a dense, acrid humidity that almost felt as though it could suffocate. She heard a faint ticking, an almost inaudible Morse code, a language of sorts. The bats were preparing

for a hunt, fathers waiting, mothers arranging their
offspring in their nurseries or putting the bigger ones
upside down on their shoulders. Dolores had described
the life of the bats so very accurately. Ever since she'd
moved to New Mexico from New York City, she'd become
very knowledgeable about nature. Suddenly Joanna felt
such a longing, a homesickness, for family, for starting
life all over again. When their mother had died almost
ten years ago, Joanna had found in her home a little
essay in Spanish describing Joanna's birth, in a town
in Guatemala by the sea. She had been born with the
help of a midwife and Joanna's father. She was described
as dimpled from cheek to cheek, creamy white, like
porcelain, with incredibly round, inquisitive eyes.
At the time, her father had worked for Pan American
Airways, operating a radio, guiding seaplanes, informing
them of the weather. Joanna wondered why her mother
herself, hadn't given her the essay to read. Perhaps her
birth had had an extra special significance to her. Was
it because she was first born, or could there be another
reason? She had often sensed a mysterious sadness in her
mother, ever since she was a child, a remoteness, as if
she were enveloped in a secret that gnawed at her. Much
later, when Joanna was twenty, her mother had told
her something that was behind the withholding nature
Joanna had always sensed. The earliest memory she'd

had of her father was a big disembodied head hovering over her, smiling, a gold tooth gleaming. What a pity he had died so early, when he had been even younger than she had been at that very moment. Feeling overwhelmed by a great sense of dismay, Joanna retreated back to the outside entrance of the cave, and pressing her back hard against a rock wall, she slowly slid to the ground. How was it she could fold her legs so easily? Suddenly, she heard a jumping, a scuttling, nearby. She turned her head and saw a small dark creature, a little like a shrew, looking at her with inky black eyes with no luminosity. He was all bent, propped up as if by crutches, but when she looked more closely she saw that it was his own enormous hands, his folded wings, that kept him upright. His wings were grand, strong, outlined by white borders. Despite his awkwardness—his hind limbs splayed to the side, his nose, which seemed to be split open and pulled upward into the shape of leaves—he had an air of elegance about him. As he opened his mouth, slightly, as if to speak and revealing triangular incisor teeth, Joanna realized that he was a leaf-nosed vampire bat, just as depicted in ancient Mayan figures of Zotz, the bat deity from the underworld.

Joanna wasn't frightened. She knew that she had to be dreaming, or as her psychiatrist had once said, that she had to be in a fugue state due to overwhelming stress.

Anyway, hadn't she wanted the little vampire bat to come looking for her? Hadn't she wanted him to fly all the way from the Yucatan in far off Mexico, just for her?

Suddenly, there was a loud commotion coming from the inside of the cave. The vampire motioned to her to follow him inside. The brown bats were all returning to their roost after the hunt. The mother bats were beginning to sort out whose baby belonged to whom, so that they might breast feed only their own offspring. The tiniest of the babies looked very odd. When they moved, they led with their behinds because they were recently born, breach born, in order to protect their large hand-wings. How intrinsically organized and predictable their lives were! As Joanna stood next to the vampire bat, she realized she and the vampire were the only oddballs, the only aliens. They didn't belong there with the brown bats at all.

Come to think of it, Joanna had always felt like a foreigner, everywhere she had been: Costa Rica, Utah, California, Ohio, Florida, Texas, and even, at first, in New York City. In Costa Rica, she'd had to repeat kindergarten for running away and returning home by herself. In the first grade, also in Costa Rica, she'd had to stand on a tall stool in the middle of the whole class for continuously poking her pencil into her hands as if she were trying to make holes in them. In Utah, when she was suppose to stand up to salute the flag, she'd stayed seated. In California, in the fourth grade, she'd hung out with a runny-nosed, bedraggled boy who everyone mocked for playing with himself. In Ohio, in the sixth grade, she had torn up a "personality book" when it had been her turn to write comments about her classmates, because she'd seen "Dirty Jew" written on Sonia Cohen's page. In Florida, in the eighth grade, she had gotten into a fight with some popular girls, who were gossiping about a classmate who supposedly ran around naked in front of her father in her own house. In Texas, in the ninth grade, she pretended to be all Mexican when she was in the Mexican class and pretended to be non-Mexican in the Anglo class. In New York City, when she had gotten married at seventeen, she'd had to pretend she was single, or else she'd have had to finish high school at night. As a model, also in her teens, she'd acted as if she were a woman of the world, when in reality, she was gullible, naïve, even stupid at times. It was a wonder she'd ever gone on to become a teacher, a guidance counselor, a psychotherapist.

Suddenly, in the cave in New Mexico, Joanna smelled something like ammonia in the air, and it was choking her, bleaching livid white spots on her arms and hands. She felt as if she were drowning in a lake of bad air. Had she finally gotten to the bottom of the cenote? Coughing violently, losing sight of the little vampire, Joanna rushed out of the cave, continuing to cough till she thought she had ripped out her throat. Where was her little friend? She didn't see him anywhere. When she had recovered sufficiently, she began to descend the many steps to the plateau below, no longer spry and limber, baby-stepping downward all the way. She walked slowly on the winding path leading to the parking lot, past the bench where she had sat in the afternoon, stumbling over uneven ground. She finally reached her car, and saw she had a ticket for not leaving at sunset. She got into the car, immediately turning on her headlights. There in front of her, hanging on the fence, she saw a white form. No, it couldn't be! She got out of the car, leaving the headlights on and rushed up to the fence. There was the little vampire bat, totally white, bleached by the urinary ammonia in the cave, hanging upside down by his hand-claws, both stiff wings stretched out to the side, his mouth open, once again as if about to speak.

Driving slowly back to Dolores's house, Joanna couldn't stop thinking of the little vampire. She was happy that she was not going to be alone. She was eager to discuss her experience with Dolores and Nick, especially with Dolores, who would understand what it was like, for a vampire bat and for her, to feel like a stranger in the abode of the brown bat. The vampire bat had demonstrated with his own life, with his own death, that she must find her own way home, wherever that was, or be as doomed as he had been. He, a leaf-nosed vampire bat from the jungles of the Yucatan, Mexico, could not become a brown bat from *New* Mexico. He could only be who he was or die.

# An Embrace in Stone

N igel, an old friend of James's invited Joanna to visit him and his new wife Vera for a weekend. Since she was going to be in England anyway, visiting her sister Ana, Nigel thought she would like to see Vera's work, her sculptures in stone and marble. He sent her photos of her statues as an inducement. Joanna didn't feel like going anywhere. She felt the shadow of a rheumatoid arthritis flare-up. However, for the moment, she was in remission. She wanted to say "no" to Nigel's invitation, but the stone figures in the photos beckoned to her in an inexplicable way. Before long, she was on her way to the home of Nigel and Vera, a reconverted barn deep in the countryside of England, up north, near the Scottish border.

On the airplane from New York City to London, Joanna did what she always loved to do, to sit by the window, buckled up, not even getting up once. She loved this time when life seemed to be suspended. It was a little like the time before birth or after death, but with the advantage of being conscious, of being able to think. In a way, she wished that she too could start again, like Nigel was doing, after losing a loved one. Actually, she didn't even know what starting again meant. She had known James almost forty years. He'd been dead for two years, and she felt as if he were just away on a business trip. She hadn't even put a tombstone on his grave yet. That would have made death totally permanent.

All of her life she had found it difficult to let go of anything—a dress, a pet, a house, a person she loved, and special toys, of course, very early on. She remembered her ten headless soldiers, which she negotiated so hard to get when she was five years old, in San José, Costa Rica. She gave the little raggedy boy, on the other side of her wrought-iron fence, her teddy bear and her clown in exchange. She immediately set to work to create heads from chewing gum. Planning to give ten figures a different face, she decided to hide them from her parents, knowing that they wouldn't like her deformed little people. But one of the maids told on her.

"I'm very disappointed in you," her father began, as they sat in her playroom before he would conduct a lesson on time and the reading of the clock. "You gave up playing with childish toys long ago. Why would you be interested in toy soldiers, of all things, and without heads!"

"I want to make nice heads for them. I want to make nice faces for them. I want them to see, hear, smell, and talk all on their own."

"But they're soldiers! Do you want them to fight, too! That's not nice, you should know that!"

"Yes, I want them to fight, if they need to!"

In the end, the ten headless soldiers were forcibly taken away. Joanna cried for weeks, seeing the dismal creatures in her dreams, looking for their heads, their faces blaming her, reproaching her bitterly.

In the old barn in England, the guestroom assigned to Joanna belonged to Vera's teenage son, Graham. The walls were covered with brightly splashed watercolor paintings taped directly onto the wallpaper in collage fashion. She could almost see faces within the blotches.

"I hope you don't mind the artwork in your room," exclaimed Vera, as Joanna baby-stepped down the staircase into the darkening living room.

"It's very colorful. Is he away at school now?" she asked absentmindedly, becoming distracted by large shadowy forms all around her. They were like ghosts that didn't dare to move.

"I thought Nigel told you! Graham is away at an institution; he's schizophrenic." Seeing Joanna's questioning look, Vera continued, "I guess you know all about mental illness. Nigel told me you used to be a psychotherapist."

"Actually, since James died, I feel as if I know absolutely nothing and never have. I've never floundered around as much as I am now," Joanna answered with a little laugh as she looked around the vast, dark space for a place to sit. The cold stone floor was causing a twinge in her ankles and knees, something like a miniscule electrical wave of pain touching her from afar.

Vera gestured towards some leather chairs surrounding a dead looking fireplace, "You'll have to forgive us. We're both so busy we forget to look after the house and ourselves for that matter. Who knows, maybe I myself drove my son into his insanity!"

Joanna felt a sudden apprehension as Vera continued, speaking in a soft, plaintive voice, "Nigel, please get some wood and make a fire. It gets cold after the sun goes down." Nigel materialized out of nowhere, rushing out through a tall, arched doorway. He was a robust little man with a long, gray beard. He was in his sixties, like Joanna. "You know, we sometimes even forget to eat!" Vera exclaimed, still standing, patting her tiny, sparse, but muscular torso. Her extreme smallness and slenderness made her look like a girl, certainly not like a woman in her forties. "I hope our dinner is okay for you. It's very simple. You see Nigel works on storyboards for his animated films all day long and I, of course, sculpt, not only all day, but sometimes later into the night."

Gliding across the room in her severe, black leather trousers and high-heeled boots, Vera reached the other side of the room where there was an elaborate array of light switches. As the lamps and spotlights went on, Vera watched Joanna's face intently. "How fantastically beautiful! I hadn't realized how enormous they were!" Joanna exclaimed, rising from her chair with enthusiasm. They were surrounded by the giant, stone and marble statues she had seen in the photos. They were all the forms of voluptuous naked women. One was bending over, with an immense round rump providing a grand sense of balance. Another lay on her side, knees drawn up, roundnesses curving into each other, a fat baby within her embrace, almost an extension of her powerful arms. Another woman was kneeling, her upper torso bent towards the ground, arms outstretched as if in supplication. Another merely stood, one hip thrust out challengingly. Vera came over to Joanna, almost in a swooping fashion, and putting an arm around her shoulders, looking upwards towards the alcove, she whispered, "Look up, look up!" As Joanna raised her head, perhaps too suddenly, too jerkishly, a vertigo began to overcome her. As she began to sway, Vera tightened her hold on her shoulder. High up on the alcove, a giant woman stood on tiptoe, seemingly conducting an invisible orchestra below. The immense figure seemed to be wafting closer and closer, the large face intrusively near, taunting her.

When Joanna regained her equilibrium, she sat on her leather chair once again. A fire roared in the fireplace, her hand held a drink of scotch. Vera was staring at her with a knowing smile. "Your reaction is so flattering to my work! You see and feel the souls within my figures; they connect with the souls within you, the souls that make up your person, your very life! I knew you and I were kindred spirits! Before you leave, I want to show you something very special to me. I'm not ready yet, but before you leave, yes?"

"Yes, I'd love to see it," Joanna murmured, confused, a little frightened, but intrigued by Vera's remarks.

Soon, they were seated for dinner, not far from the fireplace, at a rustic wooden table, on wooden stools with no backs or arms. There was neither tablecloth nor mats or decorations, not even napkins, only huge plates with hand-painted flowers and brass cutlery with rosewood handles. After serving herself some cold potatoes, cold pork, and a green salad, Joanna asked how their son was doing, what kind of treatment was he getting? Nigel answered that it was individual and family psychotherapy, peer support group meetings, and medication to allay his anxieties, to tame his delusions. Joanna carefully centered herself on the stool, afraid she may fall off. Then she said, "You know, don't you, that schizophrenia has been linked with a malfunctioning immune system? Some of the defense cells become disoriented and they attack healthy cells, in this case, the brain cells of their own host. For some unknown reason, they mistake these cells for an invading enemy coming from the outside."

"But what could possibly cause this?" Vera asked.

"Probably stress or genetics or a combination of both." Then seeing a look of guilt on the faces of both Vera and Nigel, Joanna continued, "My disease is caused similarly. My defense system, you know, my immune system, sees a part of me as a dangerous stranger, so it goes on the rampage, attacking innocent, healthy cells, causing my chronic inflammation." Joanna wondered once again, as she had so many times, if, by some accident, her body had geared itself towards her rheumatic disease instead of schizophrenia. "I'm remembering," she continued, "all the research I did, loads and loads, when I was trying to write a book, long ago, called *Bent Out Of Shape: The Story of a Woman with Rheumatoid Arthritis*. I was doing all the research, and writing and writing, because I was looking for the enemy, the monster who had assaulted and maimed me! But, you know, even as I pointed the finger, here, there, everywhere, I knew intuitively that the villain, the culprit, the demon, lay within me! I betrayed myself by some kind of duplicitous plot from within!"

Vera spoke with great urgency, "Let me see if I understand. The 'me,' you refer to, the 'self' you refer to, is not a solitary item. In other words, the self is made up of many people, well, the shadows, the ghosts of people who influence our lives, yes?"

"Yes!" Joanna responded. "In a way, it could be a symbolic 'other' who causes the confusion of the immune system that leads to the onset of a disease. This 'other' could be the intruder, the invader, the enemy, but, of course, only in a metaphoric way."

"Joanna, I'm curious about you. What caused you to get your disease, besides genetics and all that?"

"I got rheumatoid arthritis because of love. I fell deeply in love with James and lost all my resistance, all my defenses, physiological and emotional!

"Do you really think love could be so deadly?" Vera exclaimed.

"Well, the madness of love, how it unearths lost love, ambivalent love, first love, thwarted love!" Joanna laughed. "Yes, *all* the loves!" Then she surprised herself by adding, "My father died, unexpectedly, one year after James and I got married." Joanna didn't want to once again remember her father's death and the havoc, the destruction it brought about in her life, in James's life, so long ago. But she knew that soon she would have to clarify, for herself, that period of her life, once and for all.

Vera seemed lost in thought for a long time, and then she said, "I've thought about the problem of love a great deal. I hope you don't mind my presuming to tell you anything, but I sense you and I are similar." As Joanna's eyes opened wide and she straightened her back, Vera continued, "We all know that, deep down, love for a mate, is tied up with love for a parent, but I sense you put too much importance on the love for a father. I don't know why, but I also sense you haven't acknowledged the importance of mother. You know it, but you won't accept it. I saw this when I showed you my women, my statues."

"Yes," Joanna began hesitantly, but Vera's voice became louder, more intense, "Love for father comes only after we become disappointed with mother, perhaps after we actually lose mother." Then, noticing the down-turned corners of Joanna's mouth and interpreting as an expression of disagreement rather than of mournfulness, she added, "Anyway, that's the way it was for me." Then, realizing Joanna was not going to respond, she continued, "You know, I may joke around about it, but I know I'm much to blame for Graham's affliction. I didn't do anything directly, but I was dismally permissive, allowing him to think his outline extended far beyond the actuality. In other words, giving him an inflated sense of importance which can't help but lead to a painful deflation. Let me explain!" Vera stopped when she saw Nigel nodding his head slightly, as if to tell her not to go on, but she only laughed and began again, "I probably shouldn't tell you this, but when Graham was around eight or nine, he would wrap himself around my back on these very stools, twisting himself close against me, his arms tightly around me, rubbing himself against me, rubbing himself rhythmically against me, until he was at peace. I'm not sure, but I guess he was masturbating on me. But I don't even care if he was! I didn't want to stop him. I never could deny him anything. I've always loved him so much, probably too much!"

They were now starting on their third bottle of wine. Nigel just sat quietly, looking down, lost in his own thoughts, not drinking the wine as rapidly as the women. James told her that in all the years of knowing Nigel, of working with him on animated films, he'd always been a very private, quiet man. All James knew was that he, married several times and had offspring whom he never saw.

Joanna blurted out, "Did you enjoy it too, the closeness, that is, that he needed you and that you could make him feel good?"

"Oh no," Vera exclaimed, "I just enjoyed that he enjoyed it. It made him calm and content for a long time."

"What happened? What pushed him over the edge?"

"He started running away, disappearing, not knowing who we were when he returned, accusing us of terrible things..." Vera paused, unable to continue. "Joanna, you're looking tired. Maybe you need to go to bed. It's okay with me. We both need to work tomorrow, starting early. I'm sorry; we hadn't realized this when we invited you. I hope you'll be okay. You may want to walk around. It's beautiful in every direction!"

Joanna was happy to be excused; she had the beginnings of a bad backache. A little later as she was about to get into bed she realized she had to go to the bathroom. Careful not to be too noisy, she unlatched the creaky, crude wooden door and stepped down into the hallway. On the way, she stopped to look out of a window, curious about how the backyard looked. She saw a little house among the somber black trees and guessed it was Vera's studio. Inside the studio, something large stood by the window, illuminated by an eerie blue light. It was a tall, shrouded figure. Wanting to get a better look, she edged closer to the hallway window, and as she did so, she sensed a slight movement on the hallway floor near her feet. Startled, she hurriedly sped on to the bathroom and back, without exploring any further. As tired as she was, she couldn't sleep. She'd be almost asleep when large shadows would begin to parade in front of her eyes, as if wanting her to open her eyes wide. Several times, she thought that she saw the shadow of one of her headless toy soldiers, beckoning to her, wanting to get her attention, needing her to do something. Was it to create a head, a face for him? Is this why she had wanted the ten headless soldiers, in the first place? Because they were incomplete and needed her to complete them? Because they were maimed and needed her to heal them.? Because they were warriors and needed her to empower them?

The next day, Joanna was pleased she was alone. She decided to go out and find the castle she'd seen on her way to Ross-on-Wye, on her way to the barn. She needed a long walk to work out the knots, the incipient cramps throughout her body. She was awed by the endless undulating green hills, by little paths going in every direction. After a two-hour walk, urged onward by a cool breeze from the River Wye, she arrived at Goodrich Castle, a twelfth-century fortress meant to stave off attacks by the Scots. An open well at one end of the courtyard, caught her attention, the sign indicating that it led straight down into an underground fork of the river where, long ago, prisoners had been thrown to their deaths. Joanna was drawn to the narrow, dark hole. She wanted to lean over, to relax, to let herself go, to fall. Imagining herself a helpless captive, she could feel herself falling in slow motion, the sharp stones on the sides slicing her body with a vengeance whenever they could. She could feel her battered body hitting the swirling, black river. She could feel the freezing waters engulfing her whole being. Laughing a little, she jolted herself back to reality, not liking the destructive turn of her imagination. A chill shook her whole body, and she had to struggle to maintain her balance. Oh, oh, was she about to get a flare-up? Was she once again to be repossessed, to be painfully crunched by her very own rheumatoid arthritis? By her very own inner demon? Walking downhill, back to the barn, her legs seemed to want to run away, to leave her behind, to leave her to fall on her face, all by herself.

That evening, no one ate much of the meager supper. Each was lost in his own thoughts. Retiring early, Joanna once again was unable to sleep. She felt a mounting curiosity about the giant in the studio at the foot of the garden. She needed to look at it once again, to see if it had changed. She crept up close to the window panes in the hallway and saw the still giant, illuminated by the blue light. It seemed taller than it had the night before, as if it had tossed its hooded cloak to one side and had straightened up. Was this the figure Vera wanted to show her? Joanna then deliberately looked at the spot beneath the window in the hallway, close to her feet. She saw a small form curled up on the floor, long hair spread out over the pillow, a face partially squashed against its softness. It was Vera, fast asleep. Joanna hurried back to her room.

The next day was the last day of her visit. That morning, the three of them sat at the wooden table having a hot meal: tea, toasted muffins with warm melted butter, and scrambled eggs. "I hope I didn't disturb you last night, walking around. I hadn't realized you slept under the window near my room."

Vera laughed, "Don't worry about it. Nigel is a terrible snorer!" After a short pause, she continued, "Well, it's not just that; there are other bedrooms. I just got into the habit of sleeping there when Graham still lived here and slept in your room. You see, he used to have terrible nightmares, and he needed for me to be nearby, to soothe him."

"It must be difficult for you, now that he's away."

"No, not really. No one ever leaves me! No one ever disappears! They're all in my stones, my marbles, where they will live forever. It's been that way with my father, my dear mother, my girlfriends, my first husband and now my most beloved Graham!"

"Come, let me show you what I promised to show you. I had hoped to finish it, but I just didn't have enough time. So, remember, it's not finished." Vera sprang up, taking Joanna's arm, but Joanna didn't budge, she couldn't; her legs were numb, still. Vera quickly squatted, a little in front of her, knees apart, and placing both arms around Joanna's waist, she lifted her off the stool in one powerful movement and forcibly led her towards the back door. As they walked down the narrow stone path leading to the little house, the studio, Joanna's legs slowly regained their strength. Stepping inside, she saw the immense, shrouded figure she'd seen through the upstairs hall window. Tearing the canvas off, Vera stepped back, looking at Joanna triumphantly. There stood a tall, slender, abstract structure, over six feet tall, towering over Vera's tiny frame and even over Joanna's much larger figure. As Joanna stepped in closer for a better look at the shiny marble, she saw that the structure consisted of two nude forms, facing each other, one bigger than the other, each pressed tightly against the other. Their heads were incomplete, their facial features indistinct. It was impossible to tell their gender.

Joanna stared, rooted to the spot, not moving or uttering a word, as Vera exclaimed, "It really gets to you, doesn't it? You see I don't believe in working stone to find the spirit within. I take a spirit and put it into my stone. Now, do you see what I meant? No one leaves me. They can't!"

Joanna continued to stare, an ache, a stiffness, a great pain suffusing her, enwrapping and enshrouding her from the neck down to her feet. She knew she was finally in the throes of what she was dreading, a flare-up. Her remission was over. Did she feel she'd been entrapped in a stone by someone in her life? Had she herself entered a marble tomb of her own volition? No, she knew that she herself was the tomb. Long, long ago, unable—no, refusing—to say goodbye to lost loves, she'd transformed her whole being into a graveyard where her loved ones were buried. The trouble was that they were not dead. They had been buried alive. They were still living within her.

# THE CLASPING SPECTER

She had always found a certain type of drama very exciting, the type where someone was doomed but totally puzzled by what led to his predicament. Now, here she was in the same position, sitting huddled in an over-soft loveseat into which she sank, deeper and deeper, as time passed.

She had no strength, no stamina left, losing weight with every long, torturous sigh. She had no appetite, only nausea, but when she threw up, there was only yellow saliva. The windows in the living room where she sat were boarded up; only dim bulbs burned in two dilapidated lamps. She remembered shutting off the water in all the taps because the drips nagged at her, criticizing her, resenting her every thought, her every breath, almost acting like a countdown to the end.

Once in a while, she'd stagger up, stumble into the bathroom, to look at herself in the mirror, to see if she was still there. She'd had to wedge a broken-off broom from the top of the medicine cabinet to the ceiling where a leak upstairs had loosened the plaster which threatened to fall upon her head every time she used the toilet.

So, what had happened? Where had it all begun? How had she ended up hunted down from within and without? It was just a matter of time before the door would burst open, all four locks disintegrating and she'd be apprehended and dragged off. What had she done anyway; what evil had she perpetrated? Everything was hazy now, but the overwhelming sense of guilt was unmistakable, eating at her, devouring her, sucking out all self-esteem, all confidence, all sense of identity. She had lost the feeling of being entitled to live, to thrive, to enjoy.

Noises out in the hall intruded on her. People were chatting in front of her door. She rose to her feet, fleeing to the bedroom, but at the doorway she almost fainted, her heart seeming to pound her to the floor. There in front of her, loomed a giant, spidery, dried out, yellowish fern hanging from the ceiling, reaching down to the very edge of the bed. Had it always been there, or had it transformed itself?

As she lay in bed trying not to think of the fern, she vaguely remembered living a long time in another place, a large, vibrating place. Somehow, she knew that this other place had been sold out from under her—her furniture, books, clothes, and music given away to charity, as if she had died. Did she own anything? Did she have money? How long had she been in this small, ugly place?

There was a knock on the door. She stiffened. How did they get in? The front door of the building was locked—or were they living within the building itself? Then, she wondered how she knew that the front door downstairs was locked.

Then the knock came again, this time louder and more insistent. She crept down the hall and looked through the peephole. No one was there. She crept back to the loveseat and sat there hugging a cushion. Again the knock, just as insistent as the last one. Then a kick to the door and more knocking, this time going on longer. The knob turned this way and that way, more knocking, more kicking. This time, unable to stand the suspense, she ran down the hall in a frenzy, shouting, "Who's there? Leave me alone!" There was complete silence, no movement of any sort. She stood at the door for a long time; she didn't realize how long, but now there was complete darkness in the long narrow hallway.

She wanted to talk to herself just so she wouldn't feel so alone, but she didn't know how to address herself. Who was she anyway? Oddly enough, she felt clearer in the head, not so weak, faint, and nauseated. She went into the kitchen to see if she could find evidence of who she was. Lapsang suchong tea bags. She made a cup of tea and without knowing why, she knew she wanted it with scotch. Sure enough, in the cupboard was a twelve-year-old Scotch, three-quarters full. Stoned wheat crackers and Brie with garlic and herbs were next. Rice pudding with a lot of nutmeg on top, a compote of fresh fruits soaked in an orangey liqueur followed. No greens anywhere in sight and no desire for them.

She felt better. The food containers were marked Zabar's. She somehow knew that it was a large delicatessen way up on Broadway, and simultaneously, she knew she was somewhere midtown. No matter how hard she tried, she couldn't remember how she had gotten to where she was or why she was there.

Where was her handbag? Did she have one? She left the kitchen, returned to the living room. She looked everywhere but no bag. The books on the shelves were on psychology, philosophy. *The Dilemma of Identity; The Search for the Self; Human Destructiveness; Creativity: The Quest for the Father; The Demon Lover.* She knew she knew these books but could not have said what they were about.

She looked for the closet, which was down a smaller hallway that led to the bathroom on one side and to the bedroom on the other. Looking inside, she saw a shapeless leather jacket with a hanging torn lining and a label, Ferragamo, Milano. In the deep pockets, she found hundreds of dollars—fifties, twenties, tens, and fives—but no wallet, no identification. There was no handbag anywhere, only a nylon weekend bag. On the few hangers there were black silk trousers, a black silk shirt, a gold brocade vest, purple tunic. Around the neck of the tunic hung a large beaded necklace with a pouch-like leather pendant.

Thoroughly tired, she decided to lie down, the shadowy spider reaching for her silently. Was she dead with part of her consciousness having remained on earth by mistake, marooned from the rest of her? She closed her eyes.

Suddenly, flickering forms passed across her eyelids and she sat up with a start. A dark form was on the fire escape, rustling slightly as it moved from one window to the other. She held her breath, waiting. Then the form began tapping on the windowpane in a variety of rhythms, as if delivering a message. She was frightened, but again, the intrusion made her more alert. She must find out once and for all what was happening, who was after her and why. She tried to open one of the windows, then the other but couldn't. They were jammed shut by old paint. She pressed her face against the glass to see what was out there. She saw nothing.

Then a phone began to ring. Where was it? It was somewhere in the living room. She decided not to answer it, but after the ringing stopped, she regretted not having picked it up. After all, she did need to know what there was to know.

Suddenly, she remembered the pouch-like pendant on the necklace hanging in the closet. It was like a miniature bag. She unhooked it from the hanger and took it back to the living room to look at it more closely. The beads were turquoise, carnelians, tiger's-eyes and other semi precious stones. It looked like a gentrified American Indian relic. She lifted the flap, and sure enough, there was a pocket and something was in it. She put her fingers in and pulled out a key, a strange looking key. The head of it was enormous and obviously had been made separately and then welded on to the grooved part of the key. The head gleamed with a reddish-golden radiation. She knew it was eighteen carat gold, the type used mainly in Europe. The head seemed to have a raised design on one side, but as she looked at it more closely, she realized something had been written upon the gold in tiny letters. She took it up close to both lamps, but the lights were too weak; even all the overhead lights were dismally dim. Finally, she lit several kitchen matches, and perching them on a saucer, she was able to read the words:

"Even death will not part us. Forget me at your peril."

No names, no initials. Whose key was it? What door

will it open?

The phone rang again. She ran to pick it up.

"Hello, who is it?" No answer.

"Hello, hello, hello, who's calling?" Still no answer.

"Hello, who are you calling?" This time a man's voice answered menacingly.

"I'm calling *you*. I'll be right over," and he hung up. Shaking violently she rushed to the front door and unlocking it, leaving the door ajar, she returned to wait on the loveseat.

# APPARITIONS

O ne late afternoon, after being mesmerized by William Blake's study of Job, and that of his anthropomorphic Giant Flea at the Metropolitan Museum, Joanna decided to cross the street to the hotel bar. There was one stool left at one end, near the door. As she clumsily accommodated herself on it, her neighbor, a glamorous middle-aged woman, with a luxurious fur coat draped carelessly around the back of her seat, sighed deeply, looking at her sidelong. Joanna had the impression that she'd hoped someone else would sit next to her. For that matter, she herself wished that it had been James sitting there, having saved the stool for her, having already ordered a Tanqueray gin martini for her, straight up, dry, with three olives. Over the years, he had introduced her to Jack Daniel's whiskey sours, Rob Roys, Metaxa, Armagnac and pear brandies, ouzo, grappa, Calvados, saké and all liqueurs.

Joanna couldn't help but admire the woman's thick, long lashes, the perfectly blended tones of rose upon her cheeks, the outlined red lips, which left no mark upon the rim of her whiskey glass. She must have laughed a great deal in her youth, for she had many tiny lines radiating from the corners of her eyes and lips. Joanna felt that she was probably not too welcoming of older women like herself, fearing the losses of age. Joanna suddenly missed James terribly. He would have said, "What took you so long? I've missed you my dear pussycat!" His violet eyes would have had a special light in them as he looked at her, an enveloping, all-encompassing pride.

As Joanna ordered her Martini, the woman ordered another scotch, drank it down quickly, and ordered yet another scotch, this time sipping it slowly as she looked toward the door. Joanna wanted to ask her, "What's on your mind. What are you thinking about? Are you a widow also. Had you hoped to see someone, meet someone, here at the bar?" Finally, scraping her throat a little, the woman finished her drink, tossed some bills onto the counter, and gathering up her fur coat into a large ball as if it were a baby bear, she hurriedly left.

Joanna ordered another Martini, this time on the rocks with a twist—"Sacrilege!" James would have said. He wouldn't have liked Blake's Giant Flea carrying a bowl of blood with which to quench his thirst. He always laughed at her love of the grotesque, the weird. But he would have liked Job, a man struggling to understand the trials of life. As hard as she had tried to convince him of her absolute love of him, he's always had deep doubts, suspicions, feeling that she wasn't *all* his. She thought that she had been, but as she examined her life after his death, she wondered if she had ever left her father's side or whether her father had let go of her after his death, when she was in her late twenties.

A rich aroma next to her interrupted her musings—someone lithely slipped onto the stool the woman had vacated—it was a mixture of fragrant oils. She sensed a tall form, a bright blondness. She heard the rustle of a silk-lined jacket, the clink of cufflinks upon the counter, an accented voice ordering champagne. She was transfixed, not wanting to break the spell by turning to look at him. Gradually, his aroma revealed subtler aspects, an odor she used to love, the unmistakable essence of a man who has just had sex. She turned to look at him, but too brusquely—her stool wobbled, making a creaky sound. He spun around to face her, frowning. Joanna almost fainted. What a vision of grandeur—waves of thick golden hair swept backwards, deep blue eyes, dimples the shape of crescent moons even when he wasn't smiling. He must be the man the woman had hoped to meet, probably not a proper date. She had most likely seen him before, at the hotel, perhaps with another middle-aged woman. Joanna chuckled. He was not close, not far away, but for an instant, her eyes possessed him, capturing the intoxicating allure of his youth and beauty. She blurted out, "Oh my God, you're the most handsome man I've ever seen!"

Once again, the man turned to look at her, this time more fully, his eyes luminous as he wearily examined her rings, only silver, no gems, her ethnic pendant, her coat, only silk quilt. Smirking a little, he returned to his drink.

"I'm sorry," Joanna stammered, "I didn't expect to see you, to meet you like this!"

The man laughed, a mocking, low laugh as he looked at his watch. He was so familiar—the beauty, the grandiosity, the sneering independence. Would an older woman one day marry him, turning his life around while at the same time sucking up his blood, his youth?

# UNFORGIVABLE WOMAN, THE PERFUME

Riding on the number eleven bus from the first stop on Bethune and Greenwich Street to the upper west side is like traveling backwards in time, from old age to a certain youthfulness, from crumbling townhouses and crooked cobblestones to tall apartment buildings.

Ever since Joanna had moved to a small condo in Greenwich Village after her husband died, she often took the number eleven to Seventy-Fifth Street and Amsterdam Avenue and then walked one block to her favorite Japanese restaurant. One rainy gray day, as she trudged towards Bon 75 having some difficulty navigating the steep slope in front of a parking garage, she was already savoring the steamed crab dumplings, the silky salmon sashimi, and the hot saké. She wondered what little appetizer would be given to her as a gift, always in a tiny blue plate. The waiter, Yoshi, had been giving her and James either sesame-spinach salad, lemony bits of fish, or soybeans still in their pods; he'd been doing this ever since they began eating at Bon 75 fifteen years before. And then, when she began to bring Eddie, after James was long dead, Yoshi continued with his small gifts, never ceasing, not even after Eddie also died, unexpectedly.

Looking down as always, fearful of falling, she headed for the front door of the restaurant, only to realize a second later, as she looked through the large glass window, that the place was empty, totally bare—no black tables and chairs, no spiky-leafed plants reaching for the ceiling, no paintings on the walls with mysterious calligraphic messages.

"Oh, no, no, don't tell me it's gone!" Now she wouldn't be able to say goodbye to Yoshi. She leaned against the building where Bon 75 had been. She was suddenly overwhelmingly weary. Yoshi was so fine, so sensitive; he'd reacted so differently to each of her losses, never mechanically. She wondered where he was; had he gone to another Japanese restaurant in the city, had he retired or sought another occupation? She knew nothing about him, but judging by the way he'd reacted to the two deaths, she felt he must have had many sorrows in his life. He was sad when James died, but he wasn't shocked. He'd seen him mainly as a man much older than Joanna, going from tottering steps, to a wobbly cane, to being pushed in a wheelchair. But when Eddie died, Yoshi wept, quietly, his head lowered. After all, Eddie was in his early fifties, younger than Joanna, tall, robust, full of good humor, attentive to all people around him, treating everyone with affection.

Of course, Yoshi didn't know anything about Eddie, unlike one of Joanna's family friends, who'd broken off with her when she found out Eddie was an ex-convict. As a parting present she'd given Joanna a bottle of perfume, beautifully wrapped. It was called Unforgivable Woman. Joanna could only gather that the woman thought she was sullying, maligning James's memory. Sometimes, Joanna wondered why she *was* so drawn to Eddie. Besides serving seven years in prison for drug possession and assaulting a policeman in plain clothes, he was bisexual, actually omni sexual, seeking sex in any form, everywhere, anytime. He professed to never being true to anyone, to never loving anyone except for his mother, who bore him, her eighteenth child, when she was in her fifties. But he'd won a full scholarship to a medical school, even though he later lost it to drugs. In prison, he created an educational fund for children of convicted felons. He had won the trust of all officials involved, making it possible for him to work in the library and to use a computer. In addition, he forgave his older brothers for sexually abusing him when he was a small child.

Joanna knew her attraction to Eddie had to do with

loss. Yes, of course, with the death of her husband, but even before then, with the losses experienced during the hardships she had voluntarily imposed upon herself as she cared for him at home, for over five years. She told herself she wanted to care for him out of love, nearly forty years of love. But now she wondered if she hadn't been waiting to receive something from him, perhaps some words attesting to his faith in her goodness. He was always so suspicious, distrustful, despite his adoration of her, his obsession with her. "No Stone Unturned" he wanted inscribed on his tomb. Was she just another stone in his long troubled life—hard, impenetrable, unyielding, dangerous? "Can't get blood out of a stone," his psychiatrist had told him long ago, when James lamented not getting a confession of betrayal from her. She had never committed adultery while with him, yet it was as if she had, because she felt and acted as if she had, perhaps driven by a deeply entrenched sense of guilt. Was this the basis for her attraction to Eddie? He had been convicted with trumped-up charges and evidence, which he'd refused to contest. He could have been out on probation after three years, but he had insisted on serving the whole seven years. He felt he deserved to be fully punished; he had done so many bad things, including deeply disappointing his father and mother. Maybe Joanna and Eddie were twins in sin, in shame, in guiltiness.

When Yoshi and Eddie had met at Bon 75, they had immediately liked each other, Yoshi with his long braid, Eddie with his ponytail. They bowed a little, smiling slightly, their black eyes sparkling, the Asian and the Puerto Rican descendent of the Taíno Indian. Perhaps it was carnal, Joanna thought, but if so, it was also infinitely more, as if their spirits had joined together. She could not forget the way Yoshi had wept when he'd heard of Eddie's death. She herself hadn't been able to eat anything that day, not even the delicacies in the tiny blue plate. Even the saké didn't soothe, cooling much too rapidly.

The following week, when Joanna returned to Bon 75, not knowing it would be her last time, she saw that Yoshi's long braid had disappeared. After three sakés she asked him what had happened to it. He answered, "I cut. I cut in honor of your man."

Still leaning against the building that held the ghost of Bon 75, Joanna cried, silently, within herself, for all the souls of the lost. Yoshi hadn't needed to know anything about Eddie's life. Only essences mattered. Eddie was a forgivable man.

# A Trip to Die For

What an ordeal it had already been, navigating a terminally ill eighty-seven-year-old man in a wheelchair, from New York City to the ancient walled city of Tulum on the Quintana Roo coast, of the Mexican Caribbean. But as the little tour train approached the entrance, we gaped with dismay, for there, at the foot of the gate to the walls, lay a set of steep crumbling steps. No one had said anything about them.

The cruise director had mentioned that there was no hydraulic lift on the bus taking us from the pier to the train, that my husband would have to be manually lifted on and off the bus. They had mentioned that there was a short train ride from the final bus stop to the ruins. We had also known that even getting from the ship to the ferry would be back breaking because of the heavily ridged, swaying ramp. Equally daunting information had been that our wheelchair wouldn't fit through the doorway to our stateroom, so that as it turned out, our home health aide, who was traveling with us, would have to lift my husband out of his wheelchair, place his frail arms around his own strong neck, and face-to-face walk backwards into the room, holding the ravaged body by the waist as if they were doing a slow dance. Even negotiating the transfer from the wheelchair to the gurney in the airplane itself, so as to move up and down the aisles to our seats, had not been easy, but it had at least been a matter of strength and of knowledge of body mechanics on the part of our aide.

So, especially after having surmounted so many obstacles, the impediment of the ancient steps left us more than deeply disappointed.

As I write this, a few weeks after the trip, my husband cries out in pain from our bedroom nearby. He is only being washed by our faithful aide, but my husband's skin, muscles, and bones can no longer endure the slightest human touch, yearning to be left alone to merge with the ultimate, non-intrusive quiet of infinity.

At the time that we planned this trip, we were only thinking of how we could get out of our Manhattan apartment to give my husband a change from merely lying in our king-size bed in our yellow bedroom. We first thought of renting a car and observing autumn in New England. Then, when that seemed too pedestrian, we considered a week-end cruise to Bermuda, leaving from a nearby Westside dock. But because of the onset of winter, there was only one more scheduled cruise, and it was totally booked.

However, there were plenty of cruises leaving from Miami, which we hadn't considered, because the problems of flying at high altitudes with my husband's congestive heart failure necessitated a precautionary oxygen tank, prescribed by his physician.

Foolhardy as it may seem, we ended up booking an upper-level stateroom with a private verandah on a popular ship sailing from Miami to Key West and on to the Mexican Island of Cozumel.

Trying to overcome our disappointment at the unexpected flight of steps to the Temples, we devised a plan. At least two members of our trio could take turns visiting the temples above, taking photos, and preparing verbal descriptions for my husband's vicarious pleasure.

Our aide went first, leaving us in the hot sun, for there was no shade anywhere. A woman vendor offered an enormous straw hat to protect my husband's delicate pink baldness appearing above his long white hair and beard, which we quickly refused, taking for granted she was trying to sell it to us.

As we drank a little of our warm bottled water, we chatted about how good it was to have come even this close to the temples, how fortunate we had been to have seen the other Mayan ruins at Chitchén Itzá and Uxmal when we were younger and healthier and had gotten permission to do stone rubbings of the bas-reliefs because my husband was an artist as well as an aficionado of archaeology.

After the passage of perhaps a quarter of an hour, three small Mexicans in khaki Bermuda shorts and matching shirts approached us, asking in broken English if we didn't want to see the ruins. I was able to explain our predicament in Spanish since I had spent my early childhood in central America. Although I am half Mexican and a quarter Mayan Indian, I hardly ever think of myself as such, mainly because most people think I look only Irish, especially since as I age a white-pink bloat inundates the high cheek bones and the square temples.

After listening to me quietly, as though they barely understood my Spanish, one of the three asked again if we didn't want to see the ruins, that they could lift the wheelchair. Emboldened by impatience, I answered emphatically, "Yes!" and "How much?" They answered that since they were government archaeological guides, there was no charge.

With great care and a surprising strength, they lifted the wheelchair, with my husband in it, all the way up the gateway, in what seemed like one gliding movement. One of the guides stayed with us to push the wheelchair and to show us around. Before long, our steadfast aide joined us, overjoyed that we had miraculously made it up.

The grassy terrain was rocky and bumpy, but the warm breezes descending from the vast blue sky and the Caribbean Sea nearby, gently swayed the palm trees scattered here and there among the temples.

There are few joys that can compare to what I felt seeing 'my tattered lion'—as I affectionately call my husband—visiting the ruins of a grandness long gone, of carved, winged, descending Gods who represent the setting sun, of elegantly robed, masked, painted, and bejeweled priests presiding over all that is earthly as well as all that is ethereal. Ironically, we knew these carvings and frescoes were there, though we couldn't come anywhere close to them. They, too, needed to be protected against human touch.

It was all a memorial, as well as a eulogy, to my dear husband, without his having to be dead to receive it.

# S P U Y T E N   D U Y V I L

*Meeting Eyes Bindery*
*Triton*
*Lithic Scatter*